CARNY
SHORT STORIES
VOLUME 1

FIC TOM
Tomas, S. E., author.
Carny Short Stories. Volume 1.

ALSO BY S.E. TOMAS

Crackilton
Squeegee Kid

Carny

short stories volume 1

S.E. Tomas

TORONTO'S STREET AUTHOR

Copyright © 2017 by S.E. Tomas
All rights reserved.

ISBN: 978-1-7751416-5-5

For John Knowlton & family

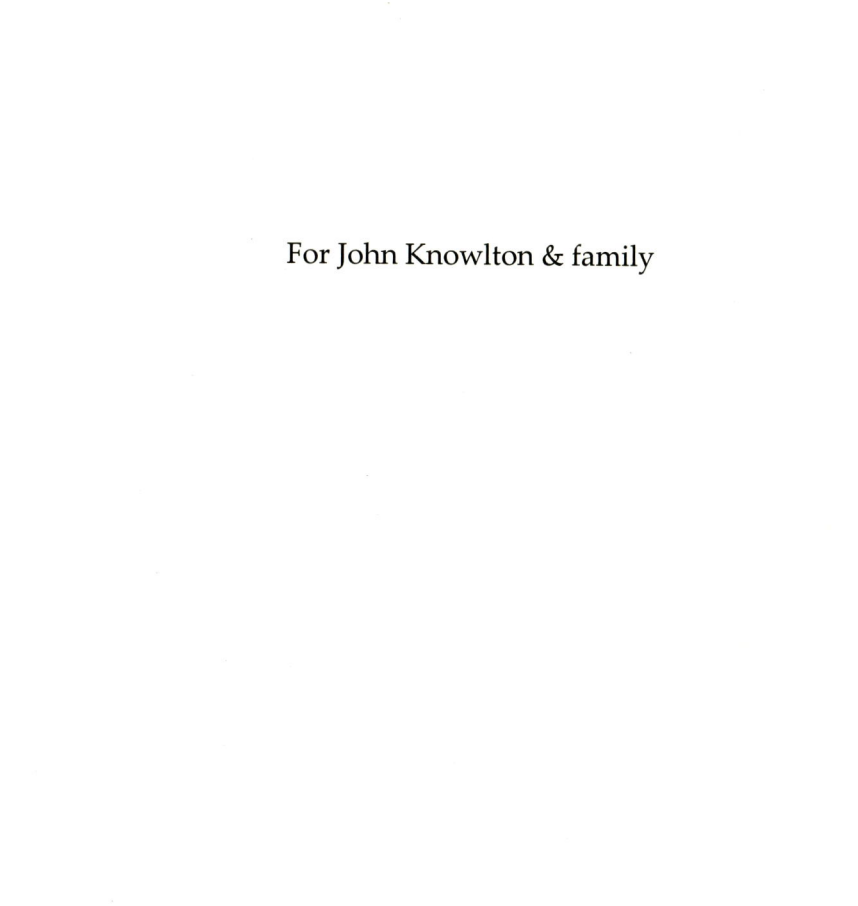

This book depicts what it was like on the carnival many years ago. The stories are based on my own personal experiences. They're essentially the highlights of my first carnival season, and of the time I spent in Florida after my first season ended.

CONTENTS

Crumpled Twenty *1*

All You Can Drink *13*

Trouble on Teardown *21*

Indecent Exposure *27*

Border Crossing *35*

Verbal Warning *41*

Overnight Low *49*

Read the Menu *61*

Johnny's Wet Dreams *71*

Layne *81*

Petty Theft *89*

Florida Crack *97*

Brutal Setup *105*

Welding Lesson *115*

CARNY
SHORT STORIES
VOLUME 1

Crumpled Twenty

I was in Edmonton, working in the gun ball joint. I hadn't given away any stock yet, since almost nobody won the gun ball, so I thought to myself, "Fuck it, I should take twenty bucks."

Some friends of mine who'd worked on the carnival the previous summer had told me that if you worked in a game, you could tip yourself right out of the apron and the bosses wouldn't know. Ian, the manager, was in the gun ball with me. It was the two of us in there, working. I didn't like the guy, really. Something about him just seemed very shady. So it didn't bother me at all, stealing from behind this guy's back.

I had a couple of customers at my counter—a mother and her nine- or ten-year-old son. The mother had just handed me two dollars. For the smaller piece of stock, it was a two-dollar game. The kid was waiting to play.

I handed the kid the gun, which was already loaded. The gun was basically just a cork gun. There was a little cork-shaped thing screwed to the end of the ball. You stuck the ball onto the end of the gun, and as soon as you pulled the trigger, the ball ejected and flew forward.

The kid didn't take much time to aim. He quickly shot at the cups, but only knocked one of them over. The cups were made of thick Plexiglas. It was actually pretty hard to knock over all three of them with that lightweight plastic ball.

"Oh, *close*!" I said. "Want to play again?"

The mom forked over another two bucks. I put the two-dollar bill in my apron. I quickly set up the cups, reloaded the gun, and then got out of the way.

The kid missed again, of course. I could see the mother wasn't going to spend any more money.

"OK, thank you," the mother said. She started to pull her son away from the game.

"All right," I said. I smiled at the mother and her kid. "Have fun today, guys. Enjoy the fair."

The customers walked away from my counter. Before I called someone else in, I took out my money like I was counting it, looked over at Ian, seen that his back was turned, and then quickly crumpled up a twenty-dollar bill and dropped it into the back pocket of my apron. The apron had two rows of pockets—three in the front and two in the back.

Ian turned around just as I was putting my money back in my apron. I immediately called someone else in. "Hey, shoot 'em up!" I yelled.

For a while, it was fairly busy. I grossed some more money. I'd already figured out that a way to keep the customers playing was to let them lean over the counter as much as the chain would let them. The gun was attached to a chain, which was bolted to the counter. So they could only lean so far. It wasn't enough to give the person an actual advantage.

"Go ahead," I said to one guy. "Lean as much as you want, man."

The guy thought I was letting him cheat. I got him to play a couple of times before he walked away empty-handed.

Not long before I was scheduled to go on break, the office broad, Lana, came by to pick up the aprons. Lana was the wife of Marty Bennett, the guy who co-owned the company that I was working for.

Lana went over to Ian's counter first. She picked up his money. Then she came over to my counter. "Hey, Jimmy, how's it going?" she said.

"Good," I said.

I took out my money and counted it. I realized, for the first time, what I actually had in there.

I handed Lana the money. She put it into something that looked like a pencil case with my name written on it. She didn't count the money or anything. She was going to do that in the office and then write down what I'd grossed.

Lana took off to the next Bennett-owned joint. On the midway, some joints were owned by Conklin Shows. These were company joints. Other joints were owned by independents like Bennett.

As soon as Lana was gone, Ian turned to me suddenly. "Hey, Jimmy," he said.

Ian had barely talked to me all day. I was new. It was literally my first day in the joint. And even though Ian had worked on the carnival for years, he wasn't trying to teach me anything. The gun ball was pretty simple, though. I was just picking things up as I went along.

"Yeah, Ian?" I said.

"Go on your break now," Ian said.

I looked at my watch. "It's only ten to," I said.

"That's OK," Ian said. "You can go early."

Shit, I thought.

This really fucked up my plan. The twenty dollars I'd crumpled up was still in the back pocket of my apron. I hadn't gotten it into the pocket of my pants yet. I was planning on doing this right before I went on break. Ian's eyes were on me now. I couldn't exactly take it.

"Uh, all right," I said to Ian.

I took off my apron, rolled it up, and then put it on the back counter, in the corner, where no customers could reach it. There was no money in the thing now, aside from the crumpled twenty, because Lana had taken all of it. She hadn't even left me a float so that I could break a big bill. There were a lot of people on the midway, though. It was better to keep the apron out of plain sight.

Once I had my apron put away, I took off my show shirt, grabbed my regular shirt from underneath the counter, and then jumped out of the joint.

"Take an hour," Ian said to me.

"All right," I said. "See ya."

I walked down the midway and threw on my shirt. I weaved through the crowd and went straight to the beer tent. I was underage to drink in Alberta—I was only seventeen—but I walked in there no problem. I'd already been drinking in the bars in Edmonton for quite a while. I never got asked for ID.

I found my dad. He was already trashed or getting there.

"Fuck, dad, you're drunk already?" I said. "We're supposed to go on that ride. Remember that ride I was telling you about?"

There was this ride that looked pretty cool. It was this big crane with a cable on it. You had to lie on your stomach, two people side by side, in this harness-type thing, with most of your body hanging out of the harness. Then they lifted you up in the air, and then took you with another crane or whatever it was, and then pulled you all the way over, so that you were even with the crane arm, basically. And then they let you go and you just swung. It was like a giant swing.

"I think I'm a little too fucked up for that ride right now, Jim," my dad said. "We'll go another time, OK?"

It really pissed me off that my dad had already gotten so trashed. I'd wanted to go on this ride with him. I was on my break. This was my opportunity.

"Can I borrow a few bucks?" my dad said.

"Why, so you can go spend it on more beer?" I said.

"What do you think?"

"The only way you're getting money off me is if you go on that ride."

"Jesus Murphy."

"You said you'd go with me, dad."

"Can't you go by yourself?"

"No, it's a two-person ride."

"Go with someone in the line, then."

"I don't want to go with some random person in the line, man."

"All right, all right..."

My dad finished his drink. We left the beer tent and then

walked through the crowd of people over to the ride.

As soon as we got into the lineup for the ride, my dad turned to me. "OK, give me my money now," he said.

"Are you kidding?" I said. "We haven't even gone on the ride yet."

"So?"

"So, you'll get it after."

"Ah, come on."

"Why would I give it to you now, dad? You're just going to duck out of the line and go back to the beer tent."

My dad laughed. "What makes you think that?" he said.

Normally, my dad would have been scared to go on a ride like this. But because he was loaded, and because he wanted the money so badly, he hadn't tried to back out of the line yet.

Finally, my dad and I were at the front of the line. The ride attendant strapped us into our harnesses, and then we were lifted into the air.

When we got to the point where we were level with the crane arm, a buzzer sounded, letting us know that they were about to drop us. Suddenly, we started falling. Then we started to swing. It was pretty intense. I felt like I was flying through the air.

The ride ended. My dad stumbled a bit as we walked towards the exit.

"What a rush, eh?" I said to my dad.

"I feel kind of sick," my dad said.

"You'll be all right, old man."

I gave my dad ten bucks and then looked at my watch. "I don't have much time left on my break," I said. "I've got to go eat and then get back to the game."

"OK," my dad said. "See you later."

I watched my dad disappear into the crowd of people on the midway, as he stumbled back to the beer tent. The guy was a hopeless alcoholic. All he wanted was to be plastered all day, every single day.

I grabbed something quick to eat, pissed, and then went back to the gun ball.

When I got back to the joint, there was another guy in there, working next to Ian.

"It got really busy while you were gone," Ian said to me. "It's going to be two in the joint now for the rest of the day."

Ian jumped out of the game and went on his break. The breaker went over to Ian's counter.

I got in the joint, put on my show shirt and my apron. I immediately got to work, calling people in.

The hour went by quickly. When Ian came back, the breaker took off to the next joint.

When it was almost time for my next break, I waited until Ian's back was turned, and then I quickly got the twenty-dollar bill I'd crumpled up into my own pocket. I didn't wait until the very last minute this time, just in case Ian decided to push me out early again.

I got out of the joint and walked through the fairgrounds to the main road, which was 118th Avenue. Now that I had the twenty dollars in my pocket, and I had some time on my hands, I was going to go play the video lottery terminal in the bar across the street from the lot. This had been my plan all along, in terms of stealing the money. I wanted it, so that I could go play the VLT.

VLTs were a new form of gambling in Alberta. They were in all the bars in the city. I'd played them already and had even won some money a couple of times. I figured what the hell? If I lost the money, it wouldn't matter because it wasn't my money in the first place. It was the show's money.

The bar was called Fireside. I walked in the door and went straight to the VLTs. They had a whole bunch of these machines at this bar. You walked in the door and they were right by the entrance, in their own separate section from the rest of the bar.

It was a Friday night and the bar was busy. A bunch of people were playing the VLTs. I found one that was free, took the twenty-dollar bill out of my pocket, and then fed it into the machine. Because the bill was all crumpled, the machine wouldn't take it.

I tried to smooth out the creases in the bill and feed it back into the slot. But the machine spit it right back out again.

"Goddamnit," I said.

I took the bill and went over to the bartender.

"What can I get you?" the bartender said to me.

"I want to play the VLT," I said. "It won't take this bill. Could you exchange it for me?"

The bartender took the bill, opened the register, and then gave me another bill.

"Thanks," I said.

"No problem," the bartender said.

I went back to the VLT that I'd been sitting at. I sat down and put the money into the slot. This time, the machine took it.

A list of games came up on the screen. I picked five reel. This was the game I usually liked to play.

As usual, I started out feeling optimistic. I knew that my chances of winning weren't good, but I wasn't expecting to win big or anything. I was just hoping to win more money than I'd spent. If I won a lot more than that, it'd be a bonus.

On a couple plays, I got pretty close to winning. I was starting to get excited.

Within a couple of minutes, however, I was almost out of money. It didn't take long at the VLT to blow twenty bucks.

Ah, well, I thought. So much for that.

Then, all of a sudden, on nearly my last spin, I had two lines match up.

"Holy shit!" I said out loud.

I looked at the lines. They were blinking on the screen. I had double sevens. I'd just won five hundred dollars.

The machine made a noise and then spat out a ticket. I couldn't believe it. There was a guy sitting a couple of machines over from me. He looked over at me, as I pulled the ticket out of the machine. Then he went back to his game.

I took the ticket and went back over to the bartender. "I've got a winning ticket," I said.

The bartender took the ticket from me and looked at it. "Five hundred big ones," he said. "Good for you." He opened the register and gave me the money. He gave me a combination of fifty- and hundred-dollar bills.

I put the money in my wallet and then left the bar. As I walked back to the fairgrounds, I thought about swinging by the beer tent and telling my dad how I'd just won at five reel. I was excited. I just wanted to tell someone about it. I realized almost immediately, though, that it would be pointless for me to do this. My dad would only try to get some more money off me so that he could buy more booze.

I decided to just walk around the midway. When my

break was almost over, I headed back to the gun ball joint.

When I got back there, there was something going on at the counter. The two big bosses, Larry and Marty Bennett, were standing there, talking to Ian.

I approached the joint slowly.

Ian and the two bosses turned and seen me coming.

I walked up to the counter. "Hey, what's going on?" I said.

"Oh, not much," Ian said. "I was just telling Larry and Marty, here, about how you stole some money out of the apron."

"Huh?" I said.

I was in shock. I didn't know how Ian had known I'd taken the money.

The Bennett brothers looked really angry. They were big guys, too, so they were pretty intimidating when they were mad.

"Is this true, Jimmy?" Larry asked me. "Did you take money out of the apron and then put it in your own pocket?"

"No," I said.

I was just going to deny it all the way. That was my plan. I didn't have the money on me anymore so I knew they couldn't prove nothing anyway.

"I don't know what he's talking about, Larry," I said. "I didn't steal any money."

"Oh, yeah?" Ian said. "Then where's that crumpled up twenty-dollar bill that was in your apron?"

I immediately realized why Ian had pushed me out on my break, earlier. There had just been an apron pickup. He wanted to see if I'd turned it all in.

"Look, I've only got fifties and hundreds on me," I said.

"You guys want to check me? Go ahead."

"Yeah, we'll need you to empty your pockets, Jimmy," Larry said.

I emptied my pockets onto the counter of the joint. People walking down the midway turned their heads, as they walked by, and looked at me.

In my pockets, I had some change, a lighter, a pack of smokes, and my wallet.

"Let's see the wallet," Larry said.

I handed Larry the wallet. He opened it. He thumbed through the bills that were in there, and then quickly closed it. Then he handed it back to me.

Larry turned to Ian. "He doesn't have it," he said. "It's just fifties and hundreds in there. They're all crisp bills."

"Well, he doesn't have it *now*," Ian said. "He obviously spent it, Larry. He was just on break."

I glanced at Marty. He hadn't said a word yet.

"Marty, what do you think?" Larry said.

"He doesn't have the twenty dollars," Marty said. "There's nothing to talk about."

It was my word against Ian's and the bosses obviously weren't taking Ian's word for it. I was making Ian look like a fucking asshole, basically.

Maybe *they* don't even like this guy, I thought.

Larry got in close to Marty. He said something into his ear. Marty nodded.

"OK," Marty said. "You can get back in the joint now, Jimmy. Get back to work."

"OK," I said.

Then Marty turned to Ian. "As for you," he said. "I don't want you looking in that kid's apron again. Is that understood?"

Ian glanced at the ground and then looked at Marty. "OK, Marty," he said.

Larry and Marty turned and then walked down the midway.

I got back into the joint. I put my show shirt and my apron on and then started to call people in.

Some people walked in right away—a guy and his girlfriend. As I started talking to them, I glanced over at Ian. I noticed that he was giving me a dirty look.

The guy at my counter wanted to play the five-dollar game. "How many chances do I get?" he asked me.

"Just one," I said. "But if you knock 'em all down, you win the big one."

"All right."

As the guy handed me the money, I glanced over at Ian again. He was still scowling at me.

I couldn't give a fuck, really, what the guy thought. I knew I wasn't going to have to deal with him much longer. Once the spot finished, I was going to go work for this guy named Frank. Frank was the one who had actually hired me. But he couldn't use me for the spot, so he'd put me on loan to Bennett. In Regina, which was the next spot the show was going to be playing, I was going to be working for Frank in the plate smash.

I laughed to myself and then gave Ian a nice little smirk, as I put buddy's five-dollar bill into my apron.

All You Can Drink

I opened my eyes and looked around. I was in my hotel room. The curtains were drawn. It was dark in the room and I was in my bed.

Ah, good, I thought to myself. I made it back here last night.

I thought about what had happened the previous night and couldn't remember much. All I could remember was locking up the joint with Chris and Robbie, walking over to the bingo tent where the show was having a big party, seeing the two oil drums full of booze, and then having a drink. I vaguely remembered talking to these two local broads after that, but that was it. The rest of the night was a complete blank.

I'd never blacked out on alcohol before. I knew I must have drank a lot of booze in order to have blacked out. I felt fine, though. I wasn't hungover. I didn't usually get hangovers, though, even when I drank a lot.

I looked over at my buddy Chris's bed. He and I had gotten a double room for the five-day spot. We made so much money in the plate smash every day, even though I was new on the show and didn't know what the fuck I was doing in the joint yet, that we could afford to stay in a hotel every night. And it was a nice hotel, too. It had a pool and everything.

Chris's bed was empty. His shoes weren't on the floor. I figured he'd hooked up with some broad the night before, at the party.

It was about time to get ready for work. I got up to go take a shower.

I grabbed the towel from off of the chair by the desk, and went into the bathroom. I took a piss. Then I turned on the water in the shower. Once the room started to steam up, I got in.

It felt nice to be in the hot shower. The air conditioning was cranked up in the room and it actually felt kind of cold.

I put my head under the shower nozzle. I splashed some water onto my face. I turned around to get some water onto my back. As soon as the water hit my back, however, I felt a sharp, stinging pain.

"Fuck!" I yelled.

It felt like I'd just put rubbing alcohol on an open wound.

I jumped out of the shower. I got out of there so fast, I nearly slipped on the floor.

As I stood there, dripping wet, I reached my hand around and touched my back. I immediately felt a stinging sensation again.

"What the *hell*?" I said. "Do I have a cut on my back or something?"

I went over to the bathroom mirror. It was already fogged up by now. I wiped it with the palm of my hand. Then I turned around and looked at myself in the mirror from over my shoulder.

I couldn't believe what I saw. On my back were these deep scratch marks. They were on the right and left sides of my back.

"Holy fuck," I said.

I tried to jog my memory. I tried to remember if I'd fucked one of those broads I'd met at the party the night before. It wasn't like in the movies, though, where the flashbacks started to come. I still couldn't remember a goddamn thing.

I had to take care of these wounds now. I didn't have a first aid kit or anything, so the only thing I could use to clean them was soap and water.

I turned the water temperature down in the shower and then got back in. I picked up the bar of soap that was in there, rubbed it in between my hands, worked up a big lather, and then started to wash my back. The soap stung. It stung more intensely than the hot water.

I washed the rest of my body and then got out and dried myself off. I tried to pat myself lightly with the towel, but whatever scab had started to form over the cuts had gotten washed away by the hot water and the soap, and when I was done drying off, there were blood splotches all over the white fluffy towel.

I turned off the light in the bathroom and then went back into the room. I draped the blood-stained towel over the back of the chair, and then immediately got dressed. I didn't turn on the TV or hang out in the room at all. I didn't have time. I just threw on my show shirt and a pair of pants, put my shoes on, and then got out of there.

The hotel in Regina was quite a ways from the lot. I had to take a cab there.

There were a couple of taxis waiting right outside the entrance to the hotel. I got into one of them. "Take me to the fairgrounds," I said.

The cabbie drove me over to the lot.

"Where do you want me to let you off?" the cabbie said.

"By the main gate," I said.

The cabbie pulled into the parking lot outside the main gate.

I paid the fare. "Keep the change," I said.

I got out of the cab and then walked towards the gate. There was a security guard there.

"I'm with the show," I said.

The guy didn't ask to see my show ID. He just let me walk right through.

I walked over to the plate smash.

When I got to the joint, Chris and Robbie were already there. Robbie was also new on the show. He'd started in Edmonton like I had.

Chris started telling me and Robbie about some broad he'd fucked the night before, after the party. When he was done telling his story, he asked me what had happened to me. "I saw you talking to two local broads," he said. "I thought maybe you took one of them back to the hotel room or something."

"I don't know *what* I did last night," I said. "I remember the two broads, but after that, it's all one big blank."

"You must have really hit the oil drum."

"I guess so."

"I know *I* fucking did," Robbie said. "I'm so fucking hungover."

The three of us talked a bit more about the party. Nothing Chris or Robbie said, though, triggered any memories for me.

"All right," Chris said. "Let's open up the joint now."

The three of us took off our shirts. It was hot outside already and we didn't want our shirts to get all sweaty.

As soon as I got my shirt off, Frank, the manager of the plate smash, came by the joint all of a sudden.

"What fucking wild animal attacked you?" Frank said to me.

I knew that someone was bound to make a comment about the scratches on my back. How could anyone not? They were deep and red and raw. They looked like they were going to leave a scar.

I suddenly felt self-conscious.

Great, I thought. I'm going to have to explain these fucking marks to people now every time I have my shirt off.

I didn't make eye contact with Frank. I tried to just brush off the comment. "I don't know, man," I said. "I don't remember."

Frank dropped the subject.

Chris, Robbie, and I opened up the joint. We put our shirts back on.

As I pulled my shirt on over my head, I felt one of the cuts open up a little bit. It hurt like hell.

Man, who the fuck does that to someone? I thought.

I'd been with quite a few broads already in my life. I was no fucking superstar or nothing, but I wasn't awkward either when it came to picking up girls. And I'd never had anyone scratch up my back like that.

The broad had obviously been a fucking psycho or something.

I tried to think back to when I'd first gotten to the party. I remembered going straight over to where they'd had the oil drums. Someone from the show had brought in these two huge rubber oil drums full to the top with booze. Some broad from the show had been standing next to them. She'd been taking the money and serving the booze to people.

"What's in there, beer?" I'd asked her.

"No, liquor," the broad had told me.

"What kind?"

"I don't know. It's like all kinds of different liquors mixed together or something."

"How much?"

"It's all you can drink for twenty dollars. We're going to keep drinking until they're gone."

I remembered looking at what was going on at the party. I didn't know too many of the people there because I was so new on the show. But it seemed like the whole show had shown up to this thing. It wasn't just a party underneath the bingo tent; it was an actual bingo party. Someone from the show was up at the front, calling out the numbers, and people were sitting around at the tables, playing bingo and getting fucked up on this unidentifiable booze. Some people weren't playing bingo, they were just walking around, socializing. I noticed a few locals there, too.

I remembered giving the broad twenty dollars and then her scooping some booze into a red plastic cup for me with this big ladle. I remembered taking the first sip. I remembered it didn't taste too bad. It was like a punch. You could really taste the alcohol in it, though.

I tried to think about what had happened after that, but this was really all I could remember. I only vaguely remembered talking to the two local broads. One of them was native. All I had was a snapshot image in my mind of me standing there, underneath the tent, talking to this native broad and this other girl. That was all I could remember. I couldn't even remember meeting them.

It really disturbed me that I had no memory of what had happened at the party. I didn't know which broad I'd slept with, or where I'd slept with her, or if I'd even used a rubber or pulled out. For all I knew, I could have even fucked both of them.

I didn't usually sleep with people like that—broads who were whores, basically; who would jump into bed with any random guy they met. I usually just got blow jobs off girls like that because at least with a blow job, you knew you weren't going to knock anyone up or catch anything from them, probably.

I knew that there would be a lot more parties on the road with the carnival. This one in Regina was like an annual thing, apparently.

You shouldn't drink anymore, I told myself. It's not a good idea for you to be drinking out here . . .

Trouble on Teardown

Robbie started getting homesick in Regina. The night before teardown, he told me, as we were closing up the plate smash, that he was planning on quitting at the end of the spot.

"I can't handle this," Robbie said. "I'm done with this carnival bullshit, Jimmy. After we tear down here, I'm going back to Edmonton."

The next morning when we were opening up the joint, Robbie was really dragging his ass.

"What's with you this morning?" I said.

"You know how I said I was going to quit tonight, after teardown?" Robbie said.

"Yeah."

"I think I'm just going to quit right now."

What the fuck? I thought.

This guy was going to quit and not help us tear down,

when he'd been in the joint for four days straight, making money.

With one less person, it was going to take us a lot longer to tear down the plate smash. Before we could even start to tear down the joint, there were a bunch of things we had to do. First, we had to take down the stock from the awning. Then we had to remove the front fence. The game was fourteen feet long, but we gave it an extra five or six feet by putting a fence in front of it, since the game involved a more long-range throw. Once the fence was out of the way, we had to sweep out all the plates. Then we could start to tear down the joint. The game was only fourteen feet wide, not the full twenty-eight feet like it had been in Edmonton—we'd only put up half the joint—but it was still a lot to dismantle.

I was pretty tired from working sixteen-hour days since we'd opened, plus all the work I'd done on setup. I wasn't too happy to hear that I was going to have to work a lot longer now because this fucking guy wanted to make other people do his work for him.

Before I could say anything to Robbie, our boss Frank came by the joint.

"Hey, guys, how's it going?" Frank said.

"I'm quitting," Robbie said.

Chris, the other guy who worked in the smash, and Pete, our ball boy who travelled with the show, were standing nearby. They both turned and looked at Robbie.

"Are you fucking serious?" Frank said to Robbie. "You're going to quit on us right before teardown, man?"

"Yeah," Robbie said. "I'm out of here."

Robbie turned and walked towards the back of the joint. We all watched him in disbelief.

"I can't believe this guy," Pete said.

"Yeah, what a fucking *bitch*," Chris said. "He just doesn't want to have to fucking tear down."

"You know what?" I said. "I'm going to go take care of this."

"What are you going to do?" Chris said.

"I'm going to go back there and knock him the fuck out."

I wasn't much of a fighter. I usually only fought when I was drunk in the bar. My buddy Kurt, though, who'd worked on the carnival the previous summer, had told me stories about the show, and how things worked out there. He was the one who'd told me about stealing money out of the apron—how if you got caught, the boss would take you out back, in behind the joint line, and beat the shit out of you. I put two and two together. I figured this was the way that problems were dealt with on the show. Robbie was a bitch, and if he thought he was going to quit right before we had to tear down, he was going to get punched in the head. I also kind of wanted to prove myself to these old school guys like Frank. I wanted to earn my stripes, so to speak.

Because it was first thing in the morning, and we hadn't opened yet, I had time to go after Robbie. I immediately turned and started to follow him to the back of the joint.

"I've got to see this!" Pete said. He turned and followed me.

I got in behind the joint line. Robbie was only a few paces ahead of me.

"You're really going to quit before teardown?" I said.

Robbie turned around. "Yeah," he said. "I'm not fucking tearing down. Fuck that! That's your guys' problem."

I walked right up to Robbie. Pete stood back and

watched. Before Robbie could say another word to me, I swung hard with my right. My fist connected with Robbie's chin.

Robbie immediately fell to the ground. I looked down at him lying there, dazed. He wasn't bleeding or nothing, he was just stunned.

I turned and walked away.

Pete was howling with laughter. "How do you like *that*, you fucking bitch?" he said.

I got back around to the front of the joint.

"What happened back there?" Frank said.

"Ah, I just punched him out," I said.

"Really?"

"Yeah, it only took one shot and he went down."

Frank smiled and then chuckled a little bit. "Good boy," he said.

We finished opening up the joint. Half an hour later, the fairgrounds opened for the day and we got to work. I worked with Chris, and then two hours later, Frank jumped in and gave Chris a break.

We worked until the early evening. Then it was time to tear down. Since we had one less person, we tried to cheat a bit and start to tear down early. There were still lots of people on the fairgrounds. Most of them were on their way off the lot.

We had the ladder out and Pete was up on the ladder, taking the stock off the awning. It was a big awning. The top wasn't teepee-shaped; it was wide and sloped down sharply like the roof of a house. The peak on the awning was so high that we could hang a few rows of big stock up there.

I was standing next to the ladder. Pete was handing

pieces of stock to me, as he was taking them down.

Suddenly, this fucking idiot came walking down the midway. He looked up at Pete, on the ladder, taking down the stock. "Hey, I want one of those," he said. "Give me one!"

I could smell the booze on the guy's breath. He was wasted and looking to start something with us.

Oh, god, I thought.

I hated dealing with drunks. They were just the worst people in the world to have to fucking deal with. You never knew what they were going to do; if they were going to get violent or whatnot.

Pete looked down at the guy. "Beat it, man," he said. "You're not getting shit, here."

The drunk didn't like this too much. He whacked the ladder hard with his foot.

The ladder got all wobbly. I was standing right there, so I was able to reach out and grab it, and then steady it, so that Pete didn't go crashing to the ground.

Pete looked down at the guy. "Hey, that ain't too smart, buddy, kicking the ladder like that," he said. "See all these guys around you?"

The drunk looked around. Everyone on the show who was in a nearby joint was looking at this guy. All eyes were on him. They were staring him down.

"They're all going to jump on you," Pete said to the drunk. "So, if you want some of that, then go right ahead, bud. Kick the fucking ladder again."

The drunk clearly wasn't looking to get into a brawl with a bunch of carnies. He was just a moron who wanted a free piece of stock.

Realizing that it wasn't a good idea, the drunk shut his

mouth, lowered his head, and then turned and walked down the midway.

I watched him for a while and then seen him disappear into the crowd . . .

Indecent Exposure

It was around twelve thirty at night and we'd just finished locking up the plate smash.

"Let's go have a drink," Chris said.

"All right," I said.

"Sounds good," Darryl said.

The liquor stores were closed, of course, but that didn't matter. On the show, we didn't need to go to a store or to a bar, or to even leave the lot to get booze. We could just go to the show's bootlegger.

The bootlegger on the show was this guy named Lloyd. He was the one who took it upon himself to go to the liquor store during his hour-long breaks during the day to get booze. And he really was a bootlegger in the real sense of the word because he was illegally selling alcohol.

The bosses, of course, didn't like this. They didn't want the help getting all trashed. So all this had to be kept on the down-low. You could drink out in the open all you wanted, once we were closed for the night and we were all hanging out by the bunkhouses. But to buy beer, you had to go to Lloyd's bunk. That was how he sold it—right out of his bunk.

We walked through the living compound, Chris, Darryl, and I, over to Lloyd's bunk.

Chris knocked on the door.

"Yeah, who is it?" Lloyd said.

Lloyd was an older guy. He had a really gravelly voice.

"Chris, Jimmy, and Darryl," Chris said.

Lloyd opened his door. He looked at the three of us, standing there.

We each handed Lloyd a five-dollar bill. He gave us each two cans of Molson Canadian. Then he closed the door.

We walked away from Lloyd's bunk. We cracked open our first cans of beer, and then walked around the living compound. We were just talking to people who were out there, hanging out. There were lots of people sitting around on the steps to people's houses. Some were sitting on lawn chairs. We were all just trying to unwind after working a long, gruelling day.

The three of us finished our first two beers. Then we went back to get more . . .

By three in the morning, Lloyd ran out of booze. We went to his bunk and knocked on the door and he just didn't answer. That was how we knew he was out.

"Oh, well," Chris said. "I've had enough to drink anyway."

"Yeah, I'm pretty fucking trashed right now," Darryl said.

"The room's going to be spinning tonight," I said.

There were still some people hanging out in the living compound. We decided to turn in and go to bed.

The three of us walked over to our trailer. We were staying in one of those ATCO trailers like you'd see on construction sites. We normally stayed in hotels, but the Canadian National Exhibition was such long hours, and it was eighteen days straight, so we just wanted to be on the lot. The show had hooked us up with a trailer. They'd rented the thing off the city. It was basically just a box with windows, a door, and AC. That was it. We got some blow-up mattresses, threw them down on the linoleum floor, and just slept on those.

Our trailer was in the back of the living compound, where the bunkhouses were located. We went to our trailer, stumbled up the steps, and then walked in the door.

"Ah," Chris said, as we walked into the air-conditioned room. "It's so fucking *nice* in here."

We immediately flopped down onto our air mattresses and went straight to bed. I was so drunk and tired that I didn't even bother to take off my shoes.

I closed my eyes. Within seconds, the room started to spin . . .

In the morning, when I woke up, I was really hungover. It was the first time I'd ever really had a bad hangover before. Chris and Darryl were hungover, too, but not as bad as I was. They weren't puking. As soon as I woke up, I literally had to jump out of bed, run outside, and puke.

Today's going to be a rough day, I thought.

It was only the morning and it was already so hot and humid outside. It felt even hotter after having been in that air-conditioned room all night and then stepping outside into the blistering heat.

I went to the doniker, pissed, had a smoke, and then got ready for work.

Because it was so hot outside, I put on a pair of shorts. Earlier in the summer, I'd bought a pair of shorts from the office to wear on really hot days. They had the Conko the Clown logo on them and they were really fucking short. I would never, in all my life, have worn shorts that were this short, but it was my first year and I didn't know that if you wanted to wear shorts in the joint that they had to be black. All I'd brought with me were blue jean shorts, which was what I usually wore in the summer. You weren't allowed to wear anything like that in the joint. If you didn't have black shorts, you had to wear the show-issued ones.

As soon as I got dressed, I went to the commissary and got a coffee. I had one sip of it and puked it right up.

Drinking something hot and being in the heat was a bad idea, I realized.

I dumped the coffee into the trash. I slowly made my way over to the joint. Chris and Darryl were already there, opening it up.

We got the joint open. Frank, our boss, came by all of a sudden.

"I feel ill," I said to Frank.

"Yeah, you don't look too good, Jimmy," Frank said. "What's a matter? I hope you're not getting sick or something."

"No, I just kind of overdid it last night on the booze."

Frank was an OK guy. I could actually tell him that I was hungover and have him not give me any shit for it.

"Yeah, I've been there," Frank said. "Live and learn, huh?"

"No kidding."

At ten o'clock, the CNE opened. Chris, Darryl, and I were all in the joint with aprons. Frank was the breaker.

I tried to work, but it was so hot inside the game that I almost couldn't handle it. It was mid-August in Toronto and it was so damn humid. Even though I was wearing these dumb little shorts, I still felt way too hot.

It made me feel even sicker, being overheated. I was already dehydrated from being hungover, now I was sweating my balls off. My head was killing me. There was a lot of noise on the midway. We were on the main line, not far from the horse palace and all that. Then I had to hear people whipping baseballs at the plates in the smash. We used unfinished, ceramic dud plates. Most of the time, people didn't break them. Most of the time people missed, and the balls slammed into the sheet of metal hanging at the back of the joint. Every time a ball hit the metal, it only made my head throb worse.

Suddenly, I felt like I was going to hurl again. I didn't have anyone at my counter, playing, thank god, so I just jumped out, ran out back, found the nearest trash can and puked.

After I was done throwing up, I spat into the trash can a couple of times. All I could taste was the beer from the night before.

I wiped my mouth with the back of my hand. Then I dragged my ass back to the joint.

When I got back, Chris had a guy at his counter. The guy had a couple of kids. I didn't even try to call someone in. For the first time since I'd been on the show, I was actually hoping that no one walked in.

I worked for two miserable hours and then I took a break. Because I was sick, Frank gave me first break. Frank jumped in and then he took my place.

I knew that if I went back to the trailer that I'd pass out and that I wouldn't be able to get up at the end of my break. So instead of going back there, I sat down on the slaw box, which was a rectangular wooden box that we kept in the joint to put stuff in, like aprons, hammers, R keys—that kind of stuff.

The slaw box was near the front of the joint. It was off to the side, away from the action, so there was no risk in me sitting there. Also, it wasn't that busy yet. It was still early in the day and it was a weekday. Things wouldn't really start to pick up until later in the day.

The slaw box was so close to the side of the joint that when I sat down, I was able to lean against the side of the joint and rest my head on it.

I closed my eyes.

Suddenly, I heard someone talking to me.

"Jimmy, wake up, bud."

I opened my eyes.

Frank was standing in front of me. He had his apron on. He was holding a baseball in his hand.

I blinked a couple of times. I felt like I was in a daze.

Shit, how long have I been out? I wondered.

I hadn't even remembered falling asleep.

"Is my break over or something?" I said to Frank.

Frank laughed. "No," he said. "It's only been five minutes, man. But your dick's hanging out. You're giving everyone here a free show."

I was still leaning against the side of the joint. I looked down. My dick wasn't literally hanging out of my shorts, but because the slaw box was so low to the ground, when I sat on it, my knees were so high up that the shorts slid right down. Because I was in the smash, there was no high counter to block people's view. They could see right down my shorts.

"Oh, shit," I said.

I sat up quickly and then pulled my shorts down as far as I could get them.

Frank laughed.

"Did anybody see?" I said.

"Yeah, some mooch," Frank said. "He was walking down the midway. He stopped and said to me, 'Hey, you should tell your employee to put his dick away.' Then he pointed at you. Maybe wear some underwear next time you want to take a nap on the slaw box, eh, Jimmy?"

"It's these fucking shorts," I said.

"If you want to go back to sleep, don't sit on the slaw box, OK? Go to your trailer or something."

"If I go back to my trailer, Frank, I'm not going to be able to get up again. I'm done, man. I can't handle this today. I'm sorry, but it's just too fucking hot, and I'm too fucking sick."

Because Frank was such a nice guy, I knew he wasn't going to fire me or anything. I was in such obvious misery that I figured he probably felt that I was getting punished enough already.

"All right," Frank said. "Just take the rest of the day off, then. Go sleep it off. Come back tomorrow morning ready to work."

"OK," I said.

I got up from the slaw box. I walked through the midway to the living compound.

When I got back to my trailer, I took off my shirt, threw it onto the floor, and then collapsed onto my air mattress.

I immediately passed out and then had this crazy dream that I was back in the plate smash, asleep on the slaw box, and all these people were standing there, staring at me . . .

Border Crossing

Chris and I arrived in Niagara Falls at around ten o'clock at night. We got off the bus at the Greyhound station, grabbed our duffle bags, and then headed up to the main road.

We walked down the street a couple of blocks. Then we came to a bridge.

"Well, this is it," Chris said. "This is the border crossing."

It was a fairly small bridge. It was just a couple of lanes for cars, and a pedestrian walkway to the right of the road. Above the road was a single rail line.

Just as Chris had told me, there was nobody around at the border. There was nobody in the guard booth. There were no cars. There were no pedestrians anywhere. The place was deserted. It looked like it was closed for the night.

"Are you sure we can just walk across?" I said.

"Yeah," Chris said. "Look around. Do you see anybody?"

We went over to the bridge. There was no turnstile or toll booth to get onto the pedestrian walkway.

We started to walk across. It was pretty exciting to be sneaking into the United States. I'd never been there before. Chris and I both had criminal records with recent charges, and I was underage, so the only way to get across the border was to sneak across.

In a few minutes, we reached the other side of the bridge. We came to a small building. It looked closed. Next to it was a guard booth.

Well, here we go, I thought.

We slowly approached the booth. As it turned out, the thing was unmanned.

"See, I told you," Chris said. "There's usually no one here this time of night."

We walked right past the booth and out on to the street.

I breathed a sigh of relief.

We were in the United States now. We'd made it across the border.

On the U.S. side of the border, there was really nothing around. There was an empty parking lot and a parkway overtop of us, but we didn't hear any cars on it. It was just a really dark and desolate area.

I understood right away why Chris hadn't mentioned looking for a payphone and calling a cab once we got across the border. It didn't even seem that there was a town there, on the American side. And it was so dark that we couldn't see a thing. I was just worried about taking that road out of there and getting to where we were going.

I followed Chris down the dark little street, and then kept on walking. The plan, now that we'd gotten across, was to walk to Lewiston. Most of the show had headed to Springfield, Massachusetts, but Greg Melnik, one of the independents on Conklin Shows, was playing this three-day spot in Lewiston, New York. It worked out well for me and Chris because all we had to do once we got across the border was walk to the lot and then go play the spot. Afterwards, we could meet up with the rest of the show in Springfield. I was told I'd be working there in the ring toss.

The street that we were on led onto the parkway.

"This road is like the scenic route," Chris said. "It's pretty dead this time of night. We'll just follow this road and it'll take us right into town."

We started to walk along the road. It was dead, all right. Not a single car passed us as we walked.

At first the road was well lit, with sidewalks. We passed a hydro plant at some point and then saw a big bridge off in the distance. Then for a long stretch after that it got very dark. It was a clear night, though. In the moonlight, we could see the asphalt and the lines on the road.

As we walked, we occasionally passed some houses. Some were fairly close to the road. We could see porch lights on through the trees.

Finally, we saw the sign for Lewiston. We'd been walking for a couple of hours by this point. We kept following the road and it brought us right into town.

From the looks of it, it was just some little hick town in the middle of nowhere.

"Well, here we are," Chris said. "Come on. The lot's just down the street."

We walked down the street and then came to a big field. The show was there, but they weren't set up yet. The rides were parked on the grass, on their locations. But that was it. Everything was just ready to go for the morning.

As we cut across the field towards the bunkhouses, we saw this bar. It was right across the street from the lot. It was still open. The lights were on inside and there were cars parked out front.

"Let's drop our stuff off and then go to the bar," Chris said.

"Sounds good," I said. "I could use a drink."

We walked over to the bunkhouses. We dropped off our duffle bags and then went across the street to the bar.

The place was kind of hillbillyish. It was more of a tavern, really.

"What can I get you guys?" the bartender asked us.

"Two beers," Chris said.

"Budweiser OK?"

"Yeah, that's fine."

We paid for our drinks. The bartender opened two bottles of Budweiser for us and then put them down on the counter.

Once we got our drinks, we just walked around in the bar. It was a weekday night, the day after Labour Day, and the place was pretty busy.

We got through the first beers pretty quickly. Then we went back to get more.

"This beer's weak," I said to Chris.

"Yeah," Chris said. "American beer is like piss water compared to ours."

We finished our beers and then went and got some more.

People in the bar started noticing how quickly we were going through our drinks. "You Canadians sure can drink," one guy said to us.

At two in the morning, the bar closed. Chris and I left and went back to the lot. Neither of us were too trashed or anything. We were just nice and buzzed.

I was tired from all the excitement and from the long walk. As soon as my head hit the pillow, I was out like a light.

In the morning, everyone on the show got up early. It was time to start setting up the rides. Even though I was in Lewiston to work in a game, I'd worked it out with the show that I'd help set up and tear down rides to make some extra money. I'd never set up or torn down rides before, but I was just trying to make as much money as I could. To me, it meant more party money. The show was going to pay me fifty bucks a day to do this shit. I thought, "I'm here anyway, so why not?"

Because only some of the show was playing the spot, it was a small crew. There were enough people there, though, to set up every ride. Each ride had one guy whose job was to move that one specific ride—to get it set up and torn down. He had a crew of people, which included local help, and they all did their thing, setting up and tearing down that ride. Because I was hired fifty bucks a day, my job was to work on a ride, and when we were done, to go to another ride with another crew.

We worked all day setting up the rides. It was hard work, doing this shit. It was brutal.

At five o'clock, when we finished work, the first thing I wanted to do was go into the bar and have a drink. Greg Melnik, however, came by and told us that we were all banned from the bar. "Nobody go into the bar," he said. "If I catch any of you guys in there, there's going to be trouble. Is that clear?"

I looked around. People were nodding.

What the fuck? I thought.

The crew dispersed.

As I walked back to the bunks, I caught up with Chris.

"What was that all about?" I said. "We can't even go to the fucking bar?"

"It's a small town," Chris said. "They just don't want anyone going in there and causing any shit. It looks bad for the show, you know? They don't want something to happen in there, and then have the people here put in on the carnies."

"Good thing we hit up the bar last night."

"Yeah, that was kind of the idea."

I still thought this was bullshit. But I figured I'd better listen to what Chris was telling me. I'd just gotten to the States. I was excited to be there. I didn't want to immediately fuck things up for myself.

I knew that, soon, the week would be over and I'd be headed to Springfield.

From what I'd heard, it was a much bigger town.

Verbal Warning

The show was playing Springfield. It was a rainy, gloomy day. I was in the ring toss, trying to call people in, but I wasn't having too much luck. Because the weather was crappy, there weren't a lot of people at the fair.

A family walked by my game. They had two young kids.

"Ring a bottle!" I said.

The kids turned and looked at me. The parents pulled them along.

"Ugh," I muttered.

I was getting discouraged.

Because I worked on commission, I didn't get paid if I didn't gross anything in the game. There was no minimum wage that the show paid you if you blanked out. You literally made no money. Seeing as how it was so dead on the midway, I was just trying to get anybody I could to play my game. It wasn't working out too well for me, though.

A guy and his son walked by all of a sudden.

"Ring one, you win the big one!" I said.

The kid seemed interested. He glanced up at the stock hanging from one of the awnings.

The ring toss was in the centre of the midway, so it was a square joint with four awnings. All we had were big pieces of stock.

The kid saw something he liked. He tugged at his dad's arm. The dad turned to his son and then said something to him.

Then the dad turned to me. "We'll be back later," he said. "We're just going to get something to eat."

I watched as the guy and his kid walked away.

Man, this sucks, I thought.

I turned and looked down the opposite end of the midway. In the distance, I saw a middle-aged couple. The guy, from the looks of it, had both of his hands down the front of his pants.

Now, normally, I would have seen this and I would have thought to myself, "Whoa, what the fuck's going on there?" But I knew what this guy was doing—he was trying to get into the pockets of his shorts.

At this spot, it was usually hot during the day and cold at night. People would wear their shorts during the day, but bring along a pair of long pants, and then change into them at night, when it got cool. It was around mid-September. The weather was really starting to change. The nights were getting pretty cool.

Because it was such a dark and rainy afternoon, this guy already had his long pants on. I already had mine on, too. Being rainy and cloudy, it was a cooler day all around. It felt like it was in the low teens.

It looked kind of funny, though, the way the guy had his hands down his pants. So, I made a crack about it, as the guy and his wife walked by. "Hey, don't play with yourself," I said. "Play my game!"

The guy and his wife turned and looked at me. I couldn't tell what they were thinking. They didn't laugh. They didn't smile. They showed absolutely no emotion.

OK, I thought. They're going to walk by like the rest of them.

And this was exactly what they did. They just turned and looked at me for a second, and then they just kept right on walking.

Ah, whatever, I thought.

Finally, I got some action. A couple of boys walked in. They looked about twelve or thirteen years old.

"How much to play?" one of the boys asked me.

"Twenty-five cents a ring, or five bucks for a bucket," I said.

"OK, I'll get a bucket," one of the boys said.

"Me, too," the other boy said.

The boys forked over their money. I gave them each a bucket of rings.

The boys each went through their entire bucket of rings, but didn't get one ring onto a bottle. You had to get the ring over one of those old school Coke bottles. The bottles were on a table in the middle of the joint. If you got a ring on one of them, you got anything you wanted in the whole joint. Some days, lots of people were winning. Other days, almost nobody won. It was a game of chance. It was just a matter of getting the right bounce, basically.

"Want to try again?" I said to the boys.

"Nah," the boys said.

They turned and walked away.

Nate, the other guy who worked in the ring toss with me, came back to the joint all of a sudden. I looked at my watch and realized that the hour was up and that it was time for my break.

Because it had been so slow all day, the break schedule was an hour in, an hour out. We only had one guy at a time in the game.

Nate put his apron on as I took mine off.

"How was it?" Nate said.

"Shitty," I said. "It's fucking deadsville here, man."

"I hope the weather's nice tomorrow."

"Yeah, I heard it's supposed to be sunny."

I rolled up my apron and then stashed it in the slaw box. The box was underneath the table that the bottles sat on, so that it wasn't visible to the customers.

I jumped out of the joint and then walked down the midway. I got something to eat, pissed, and then went over by the bunkhouses to smoke a joint.

The joint mellowed me out a bit. It made me not care so much that I'd been blanking out all day. I just had a couple of tokes. That was all I needed. Then I put the joint out and went back onto the midway.

My break ended and I went back to the joint.

"How'd it go?" I said to Nate.

"Like shit," Nate said.

Nate jumped out. I jumped in, put on my apron, and then started calling people in.

Twenty minutes went by. I was getting nothing. People were just walking right by. It was raining lightly now. Nobody wanted to play the games in the rain. They were all going inside the buildings.

I looked down the midway. Some guy in a white Conklin shirt came walking by.

"Hey, Jimmy," the guy said. "Do you like being out here?"

I didn't even recognize the guy.

"Yeah, it's pretty good," I said.

"All right. Then keep your comments to yourself."

I was dumbfounded.

"OK," I said.

The guy didn't stop by my game at all. He just said this to me as he was walking by.

I watched as the guy walked off down the midway. He was an older guy, probably in his fifties. He was walking at a brisk pace, like he had somewhere important to be.

At first, I couldn't understand what the fuck this guy was talking about. What comment? I thought.

Then I put two and two together.

Oh, the *white* shirt, I said to myself.

I realized what department the guy worked in. He was from Guest Relations.

The people who worked in Guest Relations on the show wore these white golf shirts. The shirt had the Conko the Clown logo on it with "Guest Relations" written on it below the clown. You never saw these people around the games much. They only showed up when a customer made a complaint against someone in one of the joints, which wasn't very often.

I'd never had a complaint made against me before. I'd never had to deal with anybody from this department. It was only a verbal warning that the guy had given me, but it still pissed me off.

I thought about all the things I'd said to people all day,

in the game, and what could have been considered offensive. The only thing I could think of was what I'd said to that guy who'd had his hands down his pants.

I figured it had to be this guy who'd complained. I hadn't said anything even remotely offensive to anyone else all day. No one else had even been around my game when I'd said this to this guy. It had only been him and his wife.

I still thought the comment was funny. The guy obviously couldn't take a joke.

Man, what a crying little bitch, I thought. You get all offended and right away, you run right to Guest Relations and make a formal complaint?

I figured that the guy and his wife had probably walked straight there, as soon as I'd made the crack to them. It wasn't like that much time had passed. What was so odd about it was how these people hadn't even seemed that offended. They hadn't let on at all that I'd pissed them off.

The guy from Guest Relations was basically just telling me to smarten up. That was all he was saying. He didn't have to tell me that someone had made a complaint against me. He knew that I'd make the connection; that I'd figure out what I'd said.

I got the message loud and clear. I'd just been trying to joke around with the guy. I'd thought he'd have a sense of humour. I was just seeing if I could get a reaction out of him. I thought maybe he'd smile and then walk in and play my game.

You thought wrong, I told myself.

The guy was just an uptight prick.

I obviously still had a lot to learn on the carnival. I was still green as fuck. Because I worked on commission, though, I knew that if I didn't take risks and make cracks to people when I was working in the joint that I wouldn't last on the show because that was what you had to do to get people to walk into your game. If they didn't walk in, you didn't make money. If you didn't make money, you didn't last out there. So you just had to take the risk. I knew that I wasn't going to get fired over a comment. Guest Relations just had to say something to me because a formal complaint had been made. They just had to make it look like they were doing their job.

Some more people walked by my game. It was a mother and her nine- or ten-year-old daughter.

"Hey, ring a bottle!" I said. "First time you win, you win choice!"

The mother and her kid glanced at me. But they kept on walking.

"What is it, my hair?" I said.

This wasn't a crack that I'd made up or anything. I'd heard this one before. Certain cracks were OK to say. When you had somebody against your counter, though, you didn't go and work the same way that the guy beside you was working. You didn't go and take his act. But this was just calling people in. Everyone pretty much used the same type of things.

I had no hair. That was the joke, here. I had a shaved head.

The broad and her daughter turned and looked at me. I got a reaction from them. They smiled. They didn't walk in afterwards, but at least I'd gotten a reaction out of them. A *positive* one.

It made me feel pretty good after getting so much rejection all day. I was already starting to forget about that loser who'd made the complaint against me.

Suddenly, something caught my eye, down the midway. It was another guy, walking with his wife. He had both of his hands down the front of his pants.

The guy was really shuffling around for something in the pockets of his shorts. No matter how many times I'd seen people do this, it was still pretty hilarious to me.

The guy and his wife got closer to my joint. I could see that the guy was middle-aged. He looked like he had a total bug up his ass. His wife looked like she had a bug up her ass, too.

I let them walk by and said absolutely nothing to them.

I decided, this time, that I was going to keep my comments to myself.

Overnight Low

It was after midnight and I was looking for a place to sleep. I was on the lot in Miami and I had nowhere to stay because I hadn't been able to find a job yet. I had some cash on me, but I didn't want to spend it on a hotel. I wanted to make sure that my money would last me until I got a job and I got paid.

Because I was in a tropical climate, I decided to just sleep somewhere on the lot. I already knew that I couldn't sleep on the ground because in the States they had fire ants, so I decided that the best place to sleep was in a semi-trailer, where I'd be up off the ground.

In behind the bumper cars was a semi-trailer. This trailer was what the ride went into when the show hauled it from spot to spot. Because the ride was already set up—the spot had already started—the trailer was empty. Because it was empty, I knew it wouldn't be locked.

I waited until everyone had left the midway. Then I walked in behind the bumper cars, and went over to the trailer. The double doors in the back were unlatched.

I pulled the handle on one of the doors, opened the door, and climbed inside.

I had a sleeping bag and a small pillow with me in my duffle bag. I took the stuff out of the bag and then unrolled the sleeping bag. It was just a bare wooden floor inside the trailer. I knew it wouldn't be very comfortable to sleep on, but it would have to do.

It was starting to feel a bit cooler outside, so before I went to bed, I put on some warmer clothing. I had a pair of jogging pants and a hoodie in my bag. I put them on overtop of my pants and t-shirt, and then I put the hood up on the sweater.

I tried to close the door to the trailer as much as I could just in case somebody happened to walk by and see it open. Like at any spot, the help stayed on the lot in the bunkhouses and the bosses were in their houses trailers. The living quarters were in the parking lot, but you never knew who could come walking by on the lot.

I got into my sleeping bag. I zipped it up and then went right to sleep.

I slept for a couple of hours. Then I woke up, suddenly. I found myself curled up in a little ball. I was shivering.

What the hell? I thought.

I couldn't believe the temperature had dropped this low in Miami.

I didn't have any other warm clothing with me, so the only thing I could do to keep warm was to huddle up in the sleeping bag. I had my knees almost to my chest, but I was still freezing.

For a while, I laid there, shivering. Somehow, I managed to fall back asleep.

I slept for a few more hours and then I woke up again with this terrible urge to piss. The sun wasn't up yet. It was still freezing cold outside.

I really didn't want to get up, out of the sleeping bag. I wanted to stay huddled in there for as long as I could. But I had to piss so bad that after a few minutes, I couldn't take it anymore, and I forced myself to get up.

I didn't care about finding a doniker. I just pissed right outside the trailer, against the fence.

As I was standing there, with my dick in my hand, pissing, I could literally see my breath.

This is unreal, I thought.

I finished pissing and then went back to the trailer. I got back into my sleeping bag. All the body heat that had built up in there had disappeared. It felt like I was lying in a cold, damp sack.

I tried to sleep some more, but I couldn't.

After lying there for an hour or so, the sun started to come up. "Fuck it," I said to myself. "You might as well get up now."

I didn't want to have to haul my duffle bag around with me all day again, while I tried to look for a job, so I stashed it in the trailer. I figured it'd be safe there. I closed the door, and then headed towards the exit to Santa's. That was what the place was called—"Santa's Enchanted Forest."

I walked through the lot towards the exit. There was only one place to exit and enter the lot. There were some Christmas lights arching over a path. There was no gate. At this place, you didn't have to pay admission. When I'd got there the night before, I'd just walked right in.

As I left the lot, I noticed that there was frost on the grass. I got onto the main road, which was Bird Road, and then I headed towards the nearest convenience store. I wanted to get a pack of smokes and some snacks.

As I walked down the street to the store, I passed some people on their way to work or whatever. They were wearing parkas.

Holy crap, I thought.

It wasn't really that cold. It was cold if you were sleeping outside, and weren't moving around, but it wasn't really cold enough to need a winter coat. A fall coat would have done fine. But this was Miami, I told myself. These people obviously weren't used to the cold.

At the convenience store, the clerk was also wearing a winter jacket.

I nodded to the guy as I walked in there, and then went down the aisle where they had all the candy and the potato chips.

I picked out a few snacks and then went up to the till.

I put my items down on the counter. "Marlboro Red," I said.

The clerk put a pack of Marlboro Reds onto the counter for me. He scanned the smokes and the snacks. "Five-fifty," he said.

I gave the clerk the money. I made some small talk with him as he counted up the change.

"What's with this weather, man?" I said. "I thought it was supposed to be warm here."

The guy laughed. "This is a freak occurrence," he said. "We don't normally get frost here overnight. I can't even remember the last time we got frost."

Wow, I thought. The day I come to town and decide to sleep outside, they get fucking frost. What are the odds?

I left the convenience store and headed back down the road to the lot.

Because it was the end of October and school was in session, Santa's couldn't open until the late afternoon, when school was out for the day. The only exception to this rule was state fairs, where they could ask for ID at the gate. So I knew I had time to kill.

I had nothing to do, so I just hung around on the lot. Within an hour or so, it started to get warmer outside. By ten o'clock in the morning, it was already hot.

I went back to the trailer I'd slept in and put my extra clothes back into my duffle bag.

Later that day, as soon as Santa's opened, I started to look around there for a job. It was a pretty small lot compared to Conklin Shows. Conklin was a really big show. This looked more like the size of a small show. Only it wasn't an actual show that was playing the spot, it was just independently owned companies that were there. The place was called Santa's because it was Christmas-themed. There were lights on the trees, Christmas displays, a big Christmas tree—that sort of stuff. And it ran from October through New Year's. It was apparently seventy-two days long.

What I was looking for, specifically, was a job in a food joint. Before Conklin's season had ended, someone on the show had told me about Santa's. They'd said to me, "If you're going to stay here in the States, you should go to Santa's and work in a food trap." So this was what I was trying to do.

I realized, once I'd actually seen the place, why I'd been

told to work in a food joint, rather than in a game. There were customers at Santa's—it wasn't completely dead there or anything—but it didn't seem like the place was busy enough for somebody like me, who was new and who didn't really know what they were doing in the game. Once I'd looked at the place, I didn't think that I could make enough money there, in a joint. For this reason, I decided to take this person's advice and work in a food joint because I knew that if I was in a food joint that I'd get paid a weekly flat rate. In a game, I'd be working on commission, so if I didn't gross much money, I wouldn't get much of a paycheque. I'd literally fucking starve.

I walked around for about an hour and approached a bunch of food joints. Nobody was hiring. Then I came across two joints that I recognized from Conklin. One was Conko's Mini Donuts. The other was Conko's Curly Fries and Saratoga Chips. These joints had the Conklin name and logo on them, but they were still independently owned. The owners could take their joints to other places. Conklin didn't own them. The joints just had the Conklin name and logo because they were office joints when the show was on.

I thought that selling little donuts was kind of gay, so I went up to the curly fry joint. There was a native guy working in there.

I knew who this guy was. He was Canadian. His name was Glenn. I'd met him in the summer. I only knew Glenn as an acquaintance, though. I'd only talked to him probably a couple of times.

I went up to the window. Glenn remembered me. He just wasn't sure if he remembered my name. "It's Jimmy, right?" he said.

"Yeah," I said. "Jim."

"So, you're working here now?"

"I'm trying to. I just got here last night. I haven't been able to find a job yet."

"Well, there's nothing available here right now. But I think they might be getting rid of somebody soon."

"Oh, yeah?"

"Yeah, I think they're going to can somebody today."

There was another person working with Glenn in the joint. She was slicing up some potatoes. I looked over at her.

"Not her," Glenn said. "It's some new guy who just started yesterday. Some American. He's on his break right now. I don't think he's working out too well, though, if you know what I mean."

"Yeah, I get you."

"You should check back at the end of the day. I'll talk to Sam or Carol the next time I see them. You've met Sam and Carol, right?"

"No, I haven't, actually."

"Oh. Well, they're the owners. They also own the mini donuts. Anyway, I'll talk to them tonight for you. I'll see if I can get you in."

It seemed like Glenn was the manager of the joint. He was older than me. He was probably in his mid-twenties. I figured that if he could talk to Sam and Carol for me, it could really help me out. I'd never met them, but I figured that they might have known who I was on the show. They might have seen me around.

"All right," I said. "Thanks, Glenn."

"Yeah, no problem," Glenn said.

I left Glenn's window and then walked around the lot

some more. I approached some other food joints. They had all kinds of foods there—burger joints, pizza, corn dogs. I had no idea if Sam and Carol were going to end up canning that guy in the curly fry, so I just kept looking for a job. I wanted to have something else as a backup, just in case they didn't end up letting that guy go.

I talked to some bosses and stuff, but nobody was hiring. I didn't give up. I was determined to find a job. I knew that I'd find something eventually. People were always quitting or getting fired on the carnival. I'd seen quite a few people come and go in the short time I'd worked on Conklin. I just had to be persistent and keep asking around.

After looking around for a few hours, I decided to take a break. I went over to one of the little tents that they had there. There was seating underneath it.

I sat and chilled there for a while by myself. I'd recognized some people from Conklin, as I'd walked around, but I didn't really know any of them. I didn't feel like I could approach anybody or hang out with them.

By the end of the day, I still hadn't found a job. I went back to the curly fry joint. It was the only decent lead I'd had all day.

Glenn was at the window.

"Did you get a chance to talk to Sam or Carol yet?" I said.

"Yeah, I did," Glenn said. "They said you can start tomorrow."

"Really? So they canned that guy?"

"Yeah. Fucking guy couldn't do nothing right. Just a fucking dummy, you know? Carol told me to let him go. 'When he comes back from his break,' she said, 'just tell him he's done.' So that all just happened about an hour ago."

"All right. So, is there somewhere for me to stay tonight? Is there a bunk here for me?"

"We're actually not staying on the lot," Glenn said.

"Oh," I said. "Where are you guys staying?"

"At a campground. Sam and Carol have bunks there for us. The guy we just let go has to get his stuff out of there. So you can't stay there tonight. We don't have any spare bunks."

"That sucks."

"You got somewhere to stay?"

"Yeah, don't worry about me," I said. "I'll figure it out."

At midnight, when Santa's closed for the night, I went back to the trailer in behind the bumper cars. I decided to sleep there again. I still wanted to save money. I'd literally just gotten the job. I hadn't even started working yet. I needed my money to last me until I got my first paycheque. I knew I wasn't going to get paid for another week.

I knew that the previous night had just been a fluke in terms of the weather. I remembered what the clerk had told me that morning at the convenience store—that in Miami, it was a rare occurrence to get frost.

You'll be fine there tonight, I told myself.

I went to the trailer and opened it up. My duffle bag was still in there in the exact same spot I'd left it.

I was so tired from having had such a shitty sleep the night before that as soon as I got into my sleeping bag, I fell asleep quickly. As soon as I laid my head down on the pillow, I immediately passed out.

Sometime during the night I woke up. I was freezing my ass off again.

"Are you fucking *kidding* me?" I said out loud.

I was shivering and curled up in a little ball again.

I started cursing and muttering to myself, as I threw off my sleeping bag, rummaged around in the dark for my duffle bag, got my hoodie and my jogging pants out of there, and then pulled them on over my clothes.

I got back into my sleeping bag and laid my head back down on my pillow.

Watch, I thought to myself, right before I drifted off. As soon as I start working tomorrow, and I get to go to that campground, it'll be warm at night.

In the morning, I got up and took a piss by the fence. I left my duffle bag in the trailer again. Then I left the lot. I noticed that there was frost on the grass again. People on the street were wearing their parkas.

Just like the day before, once the sun came up, it got really hot outside. I had to go back to the trailer, take off my second pair of pants and my hoodie, and shove them back into my bag.

In the late afternoon, I reported for my first day of work. It was all right, I found, working in the curly fry joint. There were always two people in the joint at any one time and we switched up the tasks. We all had to know how to do everything in there. Plus, we all had to clean. I'd never worked a till before, but I was a fast learner. I was picking it up quickly.

"On the weekends, we'll always have three in the joint," Glenn told me. "It's a lot busier here on the weekends. During the week, it really only starts to pick up after around seven o'clock."

Because it was during the week and it wasn't that busy, I didn't have much work to do. I didn't have to serve that many customers at the window or cut up that many potatoes. Most of the night, I just hung out in there, snacking on fries and talking to Glenn. That was another one of the perks of working in a food trap compared to a game—you could eat the food for free.

That night, after we closed up the joint, I went with Glenn and Kelly, the broad who worked with us in the curly fry, to the company vehicle, in the parking lot. It was a Ford pickup truck that they had. A guy named Hank, who worked in the back of the mini donuts, making the batter, was the driver. Hank seemed like a nice guy, but he didn't seem all there.

Hank drove us over to the campground. It was only about a twenty-minute drive from the lot. The place was right off the freeway.

Once we got there, Glenn showed me to my bunk. It wasn't a regular bunkhouse like the ones they normally had on the show. It was actually a cube van that had been converted into a living quarters.

"You can just throw your stuff in there for now," Glenn said. "We're going to go make a bonfire."

I threw my duffle bag onto the bed and then closed and locked the door.

"Every night we have these big bonfire parties here," Glenn said. "We stay up late and get all drunk. It's pretty fun."

"Cool," I said.

That night, I got really plastered on beer. When I finally stumbled back to my bunk it was after three o'clock in the morning.

I didn't even bother to unroll my sleeping bag once I got in the bunk. I just grabbed my pillow out of my duffle bag, tossed the bag onto the floor, and then got into bed.

It was a hot and humid night. I wouldn't need to be

curled up in my sleeping bag.

It'll probably be hot and humid like this every night, now, I thought.

Read the Menu

It was a weekday night, not long after we'd opened for the day, and it was pretty slow at Santa's Enchanted Forest. I was at the window, serving the customers and taking care of the drinks. Glenn was cutting up potatoes and cooking them in the deep fryer.

Finally, we got some action at our joint. Some guy came up to the window. "How much are the fries?" he asked me.

Even though the menu was written right on the window, everyone always asked me what our prices were. It was pretty annoying. People would literally be looking at me through the glass that the menu was written on and they would still ask me how much shit cost. It was like they were too lazy to fucking read.

"Five bucks for large, three-fifty for medium, and two-fifty for small," I said.

"OK," the guy said. "Give me two medium fries."

"Do you want gravy on those fries?"

The guy looked at me like I was crazy or something. "*Gravy?*" he said. "On *French* fries?"

This was another thing that irritated me about working in the curly fry. Every time I asked these Americans if they wanted gravy on their fries, they'd look at me like I was insane. It was something everyone did in Canada, though—put gravy on their French fries. It was on the menu, so I always offered it, because if you wanted it, it cost extra. For an extra fifty cents you could get gravy. But I always got these fucking looks from people.

"Uh, no thanks," the guy said. He looked at me with disgust. "No gravy."

"Do you want anything to drink?"

"Yeah, two Cokes."

"What size?"

"Oh, you've got sizes?"

"Yeah, we've got fountain pop, here."

"OK. Two large Cokes."

"Do you want ice?"

"Yeah, lots of ice."

The guy gave me the money. I put it in the register.

Then I turned to Glenn. "Two medium fries," I said.

"All right," Glenn said.

While I waited for the fries, I grabbed two large cups, put lots of ice in them, and then filled them up with Coke. I put lids on the cups, grabbed two straws, and then brought everything to the window.

Glenn had the fries ready.

"Thanks," I said.

I gave the fries to the customer. The guy took his food and left.

I turned to Glenn. He was at the end of the joint, cutting up some more potatoes.

"These Americans always get this fucking look on their faces when you ask them if they want gravy," I said.

"I know," Glenn said. "It's just not a thing down here. Here, they just want ketchup. Or mayonnaise."

"Mayonnaise?"

I'd never seen any Americans do this. I hadn't been in the States long, though.

"Yeah," Glenn said. "You've never seen them do that?"

"No."

"Well, you'll see it at some point. I've tried it, actually. It seems gross, but it's actually pretty good."

Ten minutes went by. We didn't get a single customer. I didn't really care, though, because I got paid either way. I was making three hundred dollars a week, flat rate—all under the table, of course.

Since it was so slow, I figured I'd try to amuse myself somehow. I was just looking for a way to make the shift go by faster, for a fun way to pass the time.

I reached into my pocket and pulled out this laser pointer that I'd picked up at some store on the way to Florida.

"What's that?" Glenn said.

"It's a laser pointer," I said.

"Oh, yeah, I've heard about those things. What do you do with it?"

I turned the thing on and pointed it at the ground. It wasn't dark yet, but you could see the red dot on the black asphalt.

"See the red dot?" I said.

"Yeah," Glenn said. "Neat."

"Watch this."

I moved the dot around on the ground. A little kid who was standing nearby with his parents noticed the dot on the ground. He started to follow it.

I turned off the laser. The kid turned his head to the left, then to the right. He was looking all over the ground for the dot.

"Hah," Glenn said. "Look at him go."

A customer came up to my window suddenly. It was some overweight broad in a Miami Dolphins jersey. She had her two overweight children with her.

"How much for your Saratoga chips?" the broad said.

In addition to curly fries, we also served Saratoga chips, which were like potato chips. Kettle chips, actually, is what they were. We had lots of condiments for that item—bacon bits, sour cream, ranch, chives, hot peppers, cheese, etc. Like with the curly fries, we made them in the deep fryer.

"Five bucks," I said to the broad.

"What size?" the broad said.

"They only come in one size. It's five bucks for a plate."

This was all written on the window, of course. The broad just didn't want to read.

"OK, I'll have one of those," the broad said. "And how much are your curly fries?"

Jesus Christ, I thought. Fucking *read*, lady.

"What size do you want?" I said.

"Large," the broad said.

"Large is five bucks."

"All right. I'll have two large curly fries, then."

"Would you like gravy on those fries?"

"*Gravy?*"

Ugh, I thought. Never mind.

"Would you like anything to drink?" I said.

"Yeah," the broad said. "What have you got?"

I told the broad all the drinks that we had.

The broad turned to her two kids. "What do you want to drink, Kevin?" she said.

"Huh?" the boy said.

"To drink. What do you want?"

"Oh, um . . ."

"Jenny, what about you?"

"Sprite," the girl said.

"Coke," the boy said.

"OK, one Sprite, one Coke, and one Pepsi. How much are the drinks?"

Like with the food, all of the drink prices were written right on the window.

"Large, medium, or small?" I said.

"All three large," the broad said.

"Would you like ice?"

"Yeah."

I told the broad the total for the order. She reached into her huge purse, pulled out her wallet, got the money and handed it to me. I gave her her change.

I turned to Glenn. "One Saratoga chip and two large fries," I said.

"OK," Glenn said. "Coming right up."

I went over to the other counter and poured the drinks. I brought them over to the window.

In a couple of minutes, Glenn had the food ready. He brought the food over to the window. I gave the broad her order and then she walked away.

As soon as the broad was gone from the window, I turned the laser pointer back on.

For the next half hour, Glenn and I had some fun screwing around with the people at Santa's with this laser. We never pointed it high up or anything. We didn't want to risk getting it into anyone's eyes. The guy at the store had told me that doing that could literally blind someone. What we did was just keep it on the ground. Kids would chase it on the ground. They'd stomp on it. They'd try to hit it. It was actually pretty funny to watch.

"It's like watching a dog chase after a ball," Glenn said.

"Yeah," I said. "These kids ain't too smart."

Soon, Glenn wanted a turn at holding the laser. I handed the thing to him.

Glenn started to move the red dot around on the ground. A kid who was about six or seven years old saw it and then started to follow it.

Glenn held the pointer still for a second. The kid stomped on the red dot. Glenn moved it slowly again. The kid continued to follow it.

The kid's mother was standing a few feet away from the kid. Glenn moved the dot towards the mother. The kid kept following it.

When the dot finally got to the mother, Glenn put the dot onto the mother's body, and then started to move the dot up her leg.

Suddenly, the kid lunged at his mother. He started smacking her in the leg. He was trying to get the fucking dot. He didn't care what surface it was on.

"Oh, my god!" Glenn said.

"Holy shit!" I said.

Glenn turned off the laser. He quickly handed it to me. I stuffed it into my pocket.

"I didn't think he'd do that!" Glenn said.

"Neither did I," I said.

"What a little psycho, eh?"

"Yeah, no kidding."

The kid's mother was screaming at the top of her lungs. "Billy, stop that!" she said. "What's gotten into you? What the *hell* are you doing?"

People turned and looked. They thought the kid was having a fit or something. It was a whole fucking scene.

Finally, the kid calmed down. He stopped hitting his mother. It looked like he was still looking around, though, for the dot.

The mother grabbed the kid by the arm and then dragged him away.

After this shit happened, Glenn and I kept the laser pointed directly at the ground. We didn't want any kids to see it on their mom or dad and then start beating the shit out of them.

Glenn and I saw this black guy standing near our joint. He was a younger guy. He looked like a thug. He was wearing a red bandana.

"Check this guy out," I said to Glenn.

"He looks like a gang member," Glenn said. "He's probably a Blood."

I pointed the laser on the ground, near the black dude. There were no little kids around at the moment, so I decided that it would be all right to point it a little higher than directly on the ground.

I brought the red dot up to around the black guy's stomach. All of a sudden, the guy looked down. He noticed the red dot on his body. He must have thought that it was one of those laser-guided guns being pointed at him or something because he immediately hit the deck.

"Oh, shit!" I said.

I turned off the laser.

While the black guy was on the ground, everyone turned and looked at him. I heard people muttering. They were looking at this guy, going, "What the fuck?"

The guy stayed on the ground for a few seconds. Then he got up. He looked around like he was scanning the crowd for the rival gang members or something. Then he hightailed it the fuck out of there.

"I think that's enough fucking around with this thing," Glenn said.

"Yeah, let's just put it away," I said.

Some guy came up to my window all of a sudden.

"Hey, how much are the fries?" the guy said.

I was so tired of repeating myself that I told this guy what I'd felt like telling everyone else who'd asked me what the price of something was on the menu. "Gee, I'm not sure," I said. "Why don't you read the menu, buddy? It's fucking right there in front of you."

The guy looked at me blankly. "Because I can't," he said.

"What do you mean?" I said.

"I don't know how to read."

Oh, my god, I thought.

"I'm illiterate," the guy said.

I felt like a piece of shit.

This was way worse than anything I'd done, I thought, with the laser pointer.

It was a good thing that I was working at Santa's and not on Conklin Shows, where this guy could have gone and made a formal complaint against me to Guest Relations. At Santa's, there was no Guest Relations. If a customer had a problem with you or something, the bosses could tell them to beat it, to fucking kick rocks.

"Oh, uh . . . sorry," I said. "They're, uh . . . "

I started stammering. I was just so shocked by what this guy had told me.

How could somebody be completely illiterate in this day and age? I wondered.

The guy was older. He looked about sixty.

How the fuck has this guy gotten through his whole damn life so far without ever having to figure out how to fucking read?

The guy wanted medium fries and a medium Pepsi. He gave me the money. I put it in the till, gave the guy his change, and then quickly gave him his food.

As soon as the guy left my window, I turned to Glenn. He was at the end of the joint, cutting up potatoes.

"Man, I feel like such an asshole right now," I said.

"Why, what happened?" Glenn said.

"That guy who was just at my window . . ."

"Yeah."

"I told him to read the fucking menu and then he goes, 'I can't read. I'm illiterate.'"

"You're kidding me."

"No. He asked me what the prices were and I just went off on him. He couldn't read a goddamn word, though. He couldn't even read the word *fries*."

Glenn laughed. "Oh, man, that's funny," he said. "That's dumb even for an American. I don't think I've ever met a person who was that illiterate in my entire life."

"I feel bad now," I said.

"Don't. It isn't like the guy can complain to anyone here about it."

Yeah, thank god for that, I thought.

I decided that I wasn't going to make any more cracks like that to anyone else at Santa's, no matter how frustrated I got repeating myself to these people over and over again.

When these lazy-ass motherfuckers come up to the window, I told myself, just tell them the fucking prices.

Johnny's Wet Dreams

There was this bar in Miami called Johnny's Dream Bar. At night, after they closed, they had these after-hours parties for carnies only.

One night, after working in the curly fry joint at Santa's Enchanted Forest, I decided to go to this bar. I'd overheard people at Santa's talking about it. "Johnny's Wet Dreams" is what they called it.

I think I'll go check it out, I thought.

I was curious about what went on there. I just wanted to see what it was about.

In the parking lot outside Santa's, a big van picked everyone up who wanted to go to this bar. Once the van was full, we were driven over there. I wasn't even close to legal drinking age in the state of Florida, but nobody checked me at the door.

Inside, it was dark. It was just a little dive bar, kind of

like a Moe's Tavern. I went straight up to the bar and asked for a beer.

I sat at the bar and had my drink. Not long after we all got there, the bar closed. It was two in the morning now—closing time. The people who'd been in the bar before we'd got there all got up and left.

Someone who worked at the bar started walking around the place. He started approaching people who were still in the bar.

The guy came up to me. "You with it?" he said.

I knew exactly what this meant. It meant, "Are you with the show?"

"Yeah," I said.

"OK, you can stay."

The guy didn't even ask to see my ID from Santa's, which I had in my pocket. He just took my word for it. Only someone who was with the show would have known what that meant anyway.

The guy went around to the rest of the people in the bar. Once he'd checked everyone, and anyone who wasn't with the show had left, the door to the bar was closed. It was a big steel door.

The private party started.

Within a few minutes, I turned my head and saw someone doing a line of coke right off the bar.

Whoa, I thought.

I looked around and spotted the coke dealer. He was from the show obviously, since the only people who were in the bar now where with the carnival. He was just sitting there at a table in the corner. People were coming up to him and buying dope off him.

I finished my beer, and then went over to the dealer.

"You got any blow?" I said.

"Yeah, how much do you want?" the guy said.

"Just a twenty bag."

I gave the dealer twenty bucks. He gave me the dope. It came in a little folded up piece of paper. I'd seen this in Edmonton a lot. It was a standard thing. It was called a flap.

As soon as I had the coke in my hand, I knew I'd gotten a lot for my twenty dollars. I'd never done cocaine in the United States yet, but in Edmonton, anytime I'd ever bought twenty bucks' worth of coke, the most I'd get out of it was two decent-sized lines. Just by the way it felt in my hand—just by the weight of it—I knew that I'd gotten way more than that for my money.

I went and sat back down at the bar. Since everyone was doing coke right out in the open, I figured I'd just do a line myself right off the bar, too.

I opened the flap. I looked at what I had in there. It was definitely a lot more than I'd ever got in Canada. It looked like there were probably about five or six really good lines in there.

I spilled a little powder onto the table. There were lots of nice big chunks in it.

I took my ID card out of my wallet and then started to chop up the coke. Because it was a hot climate, the powder was sticking to the card a bit.

When I got rid of all the chunks and it was all just a fine powder, I took a bill out of my wallet, rolled it up, and then snorted a big line.

With coke, the high kicked in right away.

Wow, I thought.

This shit was so good compared to anything I'd ever

tried in Canada. I figured this was because it was probably actual cocaine that I was doing. I knew that in Canada, the coke was stepped on so much by the time it got there that it was probably majority speed. Usually, when I did a line, back in Edmonton, my heart would start racing really fast. I'd get jittery as fuck right away. My heart wasn't racing that fast, though. I wasn't too jittery either. I was a little bit sweaty, but nowhere near as sweaty as I'd get when I'd do coke in Edmonton.

For some reason, doing coke always made me feel a bit antisocial. This stuff was no different. After doing one line, I just sat at the bar by myself for a while and continued drinking. I wasn't really looking to talk to anybody at the bar. I didn't even know anybody there. There were no Canadians there, nobody that I recognized from Conklin. And most of the people there were older than me. These people looked like they were in their early to mid-twenties.

I finished my second beer. I started a third one and the booze kind of leveled out the coke high a bit. It loosened me up a little bit. It made me feel not so uptight about being around other people.

I got up and started to walk around the bar with my drink. I started talking to people. I was just trying to be a little bit more social. I'd kept to myself a fair bit on the carnival so far, and I was trying to come out of my shell.

There was nothing really going on in the bar. Nobody was playing pool or cards. People were just hanging out, drinking and doing drugs.

At around four in the morning, people started to leave the bar. I overheard them talking. "The van's going to be here soon," one person said. "All right, let's get going," another person said.

I didn't care about the van. I wasn't ready to leave yet. I still hadn't finished my coke. I wanted to finish it and keep drinking.

So, I stayed in the bar. Some other people stayed, too.

I finished my coke, drank some more, and then at around five thirty in the morning, it was time to leave.

"OK, party's over," some guy said. "Time to go, people. We're closing up."

I finished my beer, got up, and then left the bar.

The few people who'd stayed all left and went off in different directions. I didn't have enough money on me for a cab, so I just started to walk.

My plan was to walk back to Santa's and sleep in a semi-trailer or something, since it was way too far to walk back to the campground I was staying at. I'd paid attention in the van on the way to the bar, so I knew how to get back there. All I had to do was get back onto Bird Road, and from there it was a straight shot. It was about a twenty-minute car ride from the lot to the bar, so I was in for quite a walk.

I was so drunk and high that I didn't even care about having to walk.

Fuck it, I thought. It's a small price to pay for staying longer in the bar.

I started to walk down the street. I walked for a while, and then found my way to Bird Road.

Because it was so early in the morning, there were barely any cars on the road. As I stumbled along the sidewalk, I noticed that I was going through all kinds of different neighbourhoods. Some of these neighbourhoods looked OK, some of them looked pretty bad. It was a main road that cut across the city, so you saw a bit of both.

Johnny's Dream Bar had actually been in what, to me, looked like a pretty bad area. In the van, on the way over there, I'd noticed that the majority of the people in the area were Hispanic and black. I hadn't seen too many white people walking around. And then there was that big steel door they'd had at the bar. That kind of told you right there that it wasn't a good neighbourhood.

Suddenly, a cop car appeared down the road. As the cop approached, he flashed his lights at me, tapped his siren, made a quick U-turn, and then pulled over to the side of the road.

I figured the guy had seen me stumbling or something. I figured he probably just wanted to see what was up.

It was a local cop who'd pulled over, not a state trooper. There was no other cop in the car with him. He was just by himself.

The cop got out of his car. He slowly approached me. "Hey, there, sir," he said. "How are you doing this morning?"

"Fine," I said.

I was so loaded, I was sure that my speech sounded kind of slurred.

"That's good," the cop said. "Where are you headed?"

"The enchanted forest," I said.

The cop looked at me like I was a whacko. "*Okay, buddy,*" he said. "What's your name?"

Great, I thought. I'm getting jacked up.

I wasn't too worried or anything because I was just so drunk and high. I knew I hadn't done anything wrong. It was just a hassle, really. And it fucking killed my buzz.

I told the cop my first and last name.

"You got some ID on you?" the cop said.

"Yeah, hold on," I said.

I fumbled for my wallet. I pulled it out, nearly dropped it, took out my ID, and then handed it to the cop. It was kind of funny to think that only an hour or so earlier this thing had been covered in cocaine.

The cop looked at my ID. Then he looked at me. "You're from Alberta, Canada?" he said.

"Yeah," I said.

"Stay here. I'll be right back."

The cop turned and went back to his cruiser. I stood on the sidewalk and waited, as the cop ran my name in his computer system.

I had no warrants, so I had nothing to worry about. I wasn't in the country legally, but I knew that this cop had no way of finding that out on his little computer system. Someone on the show had told me not long after I'd gotten to the United States that only a U.S. Immigration officer could actually look into something like that. On the show we never had to worry about that kind of shit. Those guys never came onto the lot and bothered us.

A few minutes later, the cop got out of his car. He walked back over to me. "Well, you don't have any outstanding warrants in the state of Florida," he said. He handed my ID back to me. "So, you're free to go."

"All right," I said. "See ya."

I started to walk away.

"Hold on, son," the cop said. "Wait a minute."

Shit, what now? I thought.

I stopped and turned around.

"Where did you say you were headed, again?" the cop said. "The enchanted something?"

"Santa's Enchanted Forest," I said.

"Oh," the cop said. He started to laugh. "*Santa's*."

"Yeah," I said. "It's just down the road."

"I know where it is. It's by the freeway. Shit, when you said you were going to the enchanted forest, I thought to myself, 'This guy must have a few screws loose or something.' Well, Santa's is quite a walk from here on foot. You know that, right?"

"Yeah, I know."

"OK. Because I can give you a lift over there, if you want."

I really wasn't too eager to get into the backseat of this guy's cruiser with doors that locked from the outside. But I figured that if this guy was offering me a lift, after jacking me up and harassing me, I might as well take it. I knew that it would save me probably about another hour's walk.

"All right," I said.

"OK," the cop said. "Let's go."

The cop let me into the backseat of his car. We got on the road. In a few minutes, I saw the sign for Santa's.

Since the cop was already giving me a ride, I thought to myself that I might as well ask him if he could just drive me back to the campground I was staying at. It was only about a twenty-minute drive from Santa's anyway. To get there, you just jumped on the freeway.

"You know, I'm actually staying at a campground," I said.

"Which one?" the cop said.

I told the cop the name of the campground.

"I know where that is."

"Would you mind letting me off there?"

"Sure," the cop said. "You know, that actually makes a lot more sense, to tell you the truth. When you said you wanted to go to Santa's, I was thinking, 'What the heck does this guy want to go there for right now?'"

I didn't want to tell the cop that I worked there, with the show. I figured the less he knew about me, the better.

"Thanks," I said.

In about twenty minutes, we were at the campground. The cop pulled over and let me out of the car.

"Thanks for the ride," I said.

"No problem," the cop said. "Take care."

The cop got back into his car. He made a U-turn, and then drove off down the road.

I watched the cop until his tail lights disappeared from view. Then I turned and started heading onto the campground.

So, that was Johnny's Dream Bar, I thought to myself, as I walked over to my bunk.

I was glad I'd gone.

Aside from all the bullshit at the end of the night with the cop, I'd actually had a pretty good time.

Layne

It was New Year's Eve and we were having this big party in the parking lot of Santa's Enchanted Forest. Al, the owner of Alan's Concessions, which was one of the food joints at Santa's, bought all this booze, made all this food, and dumped in probably about ten grand on fireworks.

We were all so fucking looped by the time midnight came around, and we rang in the New Year, that as soon as we started to shoot off the fireworks, people started horsing around with them and shooting them at each other. Within a couple of minutes, it turned into a full-on fireworks fight. The parking lot was huge. We had a big empty space to run around in and shoot bottle rockets and roman candles at each other. No one got hurt or anything. It was just fun.

While this fireworks fight was going on, I started talking to this American guy named Layne. I'd met him earlier on during the spot and hadn't really talked to him much, but we were standing beside each other, shooting these fireworks off at people, so we just started talking.

After the fireworks fight ended, Layne and I continued to hang out. People started to go over by where the bunkhouses and the house trailers were. This was all within the parking lot. Layne and I went over there, too. We sat down on the steps to some people's houses and talked.

Probably because I was all fucking hammered, I started babbling to Layne about how I didn't have anything lined up after Santa's ended, and how I was getting kind of worried about it. "Fuck, man, I don't know what I'm going to do after this spot ends," I said. "I've got nowhere to go."

I knew that Layne had worked on the carnival for quite a while already. He was a lot older than me. He was in his mid to late twenties. I was kind of hoping that with all his experience on the show, that he could help me get a hole or something. It was hard because I was new and I didn't know anybody, and I didn't have much experience working in the games.

"Well, I'm going to West Palm Beach after Santa's ends," Layne said. "You can come with me, if you want."

"What's going on in West Palm?" I said.

"The South Florida Fair. We wouldn't be working on the show. I got this gig there with the parking crew."

I'd never worked on a parking crew before. A job was a job, though. I figured how bad could it be?

"That's an idea," I said.

"I know all the main guys on the crew," Layne said. "I work there all the time. It's a good gig. I can get you in no problem."

"When does the fair open?"

"Not until mid-January. But it's a year-round job, the parking crew. They've got events going on at the fairgrounds twelve months of the year. So once we get there, we won't have to wait until the fair opens. We can start working right away. Then we just work until the end of the fair, you know what I mean?"

"How long's the fair?"

"Seventeen days."

It sounded like a pretty good idea to me. It wasn't the show, but at least it was a few weeks of steady money.

"I'm going to be driving up there with my friend Ryan," Layne said. "How about we swing by here the day after Santa's ends, first thing in the morning, and pick you up?"

Most people who worked at Santa's were staying right on the lot, in bunkhouses. Layne wasn't actually working at Santa's, though. That was why he was offering to come by the lot. He was just a carny who lived in Miami and who would come down to the lot all the time to hang out and party with people that he knew from the show.

"I'm actually not staying on the lot," I said. "I'm staying at a campground."

I told Layne where the campground was.

"I know where that is," Layne said. "Why don't we come by the campground, then? Just be ready and waiting at the entrance at nine o'clock."

"All right," I said.

Layne and I hung out some more. Some other people came by and Layne started talking to them. I got up and went somewhere else.

A couple of hours later, the party ended. I got into the company truck and went back to the campground.

A few days later, Santa's ended. I got paid for my last week there, and then when we closed that night, I went back to the campground.

In the morning, I got up early and threw all my stuff into my duffle bag. I left my bunk, and then walked to the entrance of the campground to wait for Layne and his friend Ryan.

I got to the entrance early. I didn't want to miss my ride. I had a smoke while I stood there and waited.

Since the spot was over, everyone from the show was leaving the campground. Suddenly, I saw the company vehicle on its way out.

The truck slowed down and then came to a stop. The driver, Hank, rolled down his window. "Hey, Jimmy," he said.

"Hey, Hank," I said.

"You need a ride downtown?"

"No, that's all right."

"You sure?"

"Yeah. I've got someone coming by to pick me up."

"OK."

"See you around."

"Yeah, take care."

Hank turned out of the campground and then drove down the road.

I watched him drive away and then I looked at my watch. It was twenty after nine already.

Shit, I thought. I hope Layne and his friend are coming.

A few minutes later, a little white hatchback pulled up. Layne was in the front passenger seat. Layne's friend Ryan was driving. I recognized Ryan because I'd met him at Santa's. He'd come to the lot sometimes with Layne.

Ryan pulled the car over. I opened the door to the backseat, threw my duffle bag in there, and then got in.

We got onto the freeway. It was heavy traffic all the way to West Palm Beach.

When we finally got into town, we got off the freeway and then went right to the fairgrounds.

Ryan parked near the trailer for the parking crew, which was near the main gate. We all got out of the car. Then we went our separate ways. Ryan went onto the lot to go look for a job on a ride. He was a ride guy, apparently. Layne and I went straight to the parking crew trailer.

The parking crew trailer was just one of those trailers like they had on construction sites. There were a few golf carts parked out front.

Layne and I walked up the steps to the trailer and then knocked on the door.

"Come in!" a voice said.

We went inside. A broad was sitting at a desk, doing some paperwork. She looked up at us. Then she smiled.

"Oh, hi, Layne!" she said.

"Hey, Susie, how's it going?" Layne said.

"Not bad. Who's this?"

"My buddy, Jim."

It was obvious that Layne was well-liked on the parking crew. He introduced me quickly to Susie, and then the next thing I knew, Susie was handing us each a clipboard.

"OK, just fill out these forms, guys," Susie said. "Then we'll get you started."

"Is it OK if we fill these out outside?" Layne said.

"Sure."

Layne and I went back outside. We stood by the trailer and started to fill out the forms.

I hadn't even looked at the form yet. I had no idea what I was being asked fill out. I read what was written at the top of the page.

Oh, shit, I thought.

It was a U.S. tax form.

I was pretty surprised that I was being asked to fill out this kind of a form. When Layne told me that he could get me in on the parking crew, I thought we'd just go to West Palm, I'd get the job, and that it would be all under the table like at Santa's. I couldn't exactly fill out a U.S. tax form. I was in the country illegally. I didn't even have a work visa.

I decided to just fill the form out anyway. I wrote down my name and my date of birth. Then I came to a problem.

I turned to Layne. "Hey," I said.

"Yeah?" Layne said.

"What do I put here? They want a fucking U.S. social security number."

"Just put your Canadian number."

"What do you mean?"

"It's the same number of digits. The numbers are just grouped differently. Your guys' is three groups of three. Ours is three digits, two digits, and then four digits. So just write down your Canadian number and group the digits so that it looks like a U.S. social security number."

"That's going to work?"

"Yeah, it'll be fine."

"OK."

I figured that Layne knew what he was talking about.

I wrote down my nine-digit Canadian social insurance number, grouping the numbers so that it looked like a U.S. number. Then I quickly filled out the rest of the form.

There was nothing else on there that I had to lie about. For my address, I just wrote that I didn't have one; that I lived on the road.

We went back inside the trailer. We handed in the forms. Susie gave us each a parking crew shirt, and then she took us outside and hooked both of us up with a golf cart and a radio.

"Layne will show you what to do," Susie said. "Basically, though, what you'll be doing is driving around to the different parking lots and making sure that everything's running smoothly. You've got a radio, so you can communicate with the other guys on the crew and with the office. If someone needs help finding their car, we can call you on your radio. Or if one of the parking attendants needs a ride to another lot, we can call you and tell you to go pick them up."

The job already sounded pretty sweet. I thought I'd have to stand around all day, in the hot sun, directing people where to park their cars. I'd never worked on a parking crew a day in my life and I basically had a supervisory job. And it was all because of Layne.

I realized that Layne really did have some good connections. He told me he'd get me in on the parking crew, and he did. The plan had actually materialized. It hadn't just been a bunch of bullshit that had never panned out.

I had no idea what I was going to do after the South Florida Fair ended, but at least I knew that for the next few weeks, I'd be working and making some money.

And that was all I wanted, really. That was good enough for me. I was living life on a day by day basis, figuring things out as I went along. As long as I had some money coming in and a place to lay my head at night, as far as I was concerned, I was doing pretty good.

Petty Theft

The guy had no idea where he'd parked his car. This kind of thing happened all the time at the South Florida Fair. The place had tons of parking.

I tried to jog the guy's memory. "The area where you parked, was it pavement?" I said.

"No," the guy said.

"Was it grassy?"

"Yeah."

"Were there trees?"

"Yeah."

"OK, I know where you parked."

The parking lot that was grassy with trees was pretty far away. It was one of the last lots. It was probably a twenty-minute walk from the main gate.

I told the guy where to find his car.

"I don't feel like walking all the way over there," the guy

said. "Do you think you could take me there on your golf cart?"

I hesitated.

"I'll give you twenty bucks," the guy said.

"OK," I said.

This was exactly what I wanted to hear. I had no problem taking people to their cars on my golf cart. I wasn't breaking the rules or anything by doing this. I could basically do whatever the hell I wanted at this job. I was only willing to do it, though, if the person offered me twenty or thirty dollars.

"All right," I said. "Hop on."

The guy got into the passenger seat. I got onto the road that took you to all the different parking lots.

As soon as we got to the grassy lot with the trees, the guy spotted his car. "That's it," he said. "It's that station wagon over there."

I drove over to the car.

Before the guy got off of the golf cart, he pulled out his wallet and gave me twenty bucks. "Thanks for your help," he said. "You're fucking awesome, man."

"No problem," I said.

I put the money in my pocket. I exited the lot and then drove back down the road.

When I got back to the first parking lot, I noticed a guy who was parking his car where he wasn't supposed to.

I drove over to the guy. He'd just gotten out of his car.

"Sir, you can't park here," I said.

"I'm police," the guy said. He showed me his badge.

"I don't care," I said. "Are you on duty?"

"No," the guy said.

"Then move your car or it'll be fucking towed. You being

a cop means nothing here. That's just your personal car."

The cop didn't argue with me. He muttered something and then got back in his car and slammed the door.

I drove away on my golf cart.

Suddenly, I ran into my buddy Layne.

"Oh, hey, Jim," Layne said. "Keep an eye out for me, will you?"

"Sure," I said.

Layne was over by somebody's pickup truck. The truck had a cooler in the back of it. Layne opened the cooler and took five cans of beer out of it. He put them into a bag, and then got back on his golf cart.

"Come on," Layne said. "Let's bring this shit back to the tent."

In behind the grassy lot was a fenced off area with motor homes and campers. That was where we were staying. We had a tent there.

When we got to the tent, Layne took the bag with the beer in it and then went into the tent. We had a cooler in there. It wasn't ours, really. Layne had stolen it on the first day of the fair. He'd just taken it so that we'd have something to put our beer in. There were so many rednecks with pickup trucks in Florida, and they would tailgate a lot—sit on lawn chairs in behind their vehicles in the parking lot and drink—so a lot of trucks had coolers of beer in the backs of them. They were easy to steal. Since the beginning of the fair, Layne had been stealing beer for us every day. The whole spot, we hadn't bought a single can of beer.

Layne zipped up the tent, and then came back to his golf cart. He reached into his back pocket suddenly and pulled out his wallet. "Check this out," he said.

Layne opened his wallet and took out a credit card.

I looked at the card. I noticed that it had someone else's name on it.

"Where'd you get that?" I said.

"I found it in someone's truck," Layne said.

"They had it in the back?"

"No, it was in the cab. The guy left his wallet on the front seat."

"You went inside the vehicle?"

"Yeah. The door was unlocked. I saw the wallet, tried the door, it opened, so I just went in there and took the wallet."

Whoa, I thought.

I wasn't into this at all. Stealing beer out of people's coolers was one thing. Going into somebody's vehicle and taking their wallet was something else.

"When'd you swipe that?" I said.

"Earlier today," Layne said.

Layne started to tell me about how he went with his friend Ryan, who was working at the fair on a ride, to a gas station on his last break. They filled up Ryan's car and put it on the credit card.

"I also bought some snacks and a few packs of smokes," Layne said. "The stuff's in the tent. Just help yourself to whatever you want."

"All right," I said.

"I'm going to get a tattoo and put it on the credit card. I know this guy on the lot with a tattoo joint. I'm going there right now. Why don't you come with me, Jim? You can get one, too."

Even though I didn't like what Layne had done, I didn't mind getting a free tattoo.

It wasn't time for my break yet, though. Layne and I always tried to stagger our breaks. We had a lot of freedom at this job. We didn't have to check in with anyone when we went on, or came back, from breaks. But we didn't totally abuse it either. We tried to follow at least some of the rules.

I told this to Layne.

"Just take your break now," Layne said. "Don't worry about it, man. It's the last day of the fair. What the hell are they going to do, fire you?"

"All right," I said. "Let's go."

We drove down to the main gate and parked our golf carts by the parking crew trailer. Then we went onto the lot. Because we were with the parking crew, we could go onto the lot whenever we wanted to.

We walked over to the tattoo joint. Layne started talking to his buddy who worked there.

While Layne and his friend talked, I went over and looked at all the different tattoos you could get. I saw one that I liked. It was Marvin the Martian.

Layne came over to me. "You know which tattoo you're getting?" he said.

"Yeah," I said.

"OK, I'll go tell my buddy."

Before the guy would give us the tattoos, he had to charge the credit card. Layne gave him the card. The guy swiped it in his card reader.

The machine made a noise.

"Sorry," Layne's buddy said. "This card's been declined."

I didn't know if the guy could see if the card had been reported stolen or not. It didn't matter, though, because he was Layne's friend. He wasn't going to do anything about it. He just handed the card back to Layne, and then Layne and I walked out of there.

"Oh, well," Layne said. "I guess it's time to chuck this fucking thing."

Layne chucked the card into the first trash can that we came to. We got something to eat, and then went over by the bunkhouses to smoke a joint. Then we went back to our golf carts.

We finished work early that night because it was the last day of the fair. I was wondering when we were going to get paid. Layne hadn't mentioned anything to me about it yet.

"We're not going to get paid for a while," Layne said. "Not until the end of February."

It was the end of January.

"Are you kidding me?" I said.

"No, it's like I told you, Jim. This is a regular job for people. The fairgrounds are open year-round. Pay day, here, is once a month. It's the last day of every month."

Neither of us had any money. We'd been living off whatever we were getting in tips from the lazy-ass people who wanted us to take them to their cars.

"Fuck, that's a long time," I said. "What the hell are we going to do until this cheque comes?"

"Don't worry," Layne said. "I've got it all figured out. We'll just go to Conklin's winter quarters."

Earlier in the fair, Layne had pointed out to me where Conklin Shows's winter quarters was located. In behind the fairgrounds was a field. Across the field, at an angle, was winter quarters.

Layne had obviously been planning on going there all along. He just hadn't bothered to tell me.

"What about Ryan?" I said.

"Ryan?" Layne said. "He's got to tear down tonight. In the morning, he's going to drive back to Miami."

"Oh, he's not sticking around?"

"No, he gets paid tonight by the show. He doesn't need to stick around. Anyway, it'll work out perfect, us going to winter quarters. At the end of February, when winter quarters ends, we'll get paid from the parking crew, and then we'll go right to Miami to start setting up for the Dade County Youth Fair."

The Dade County Youth Fair was Conklin's first spot of the season.

"What kind of work will we be doing at winter quarters, do you think?" I said.

"They'll have us work on a ride or something," Layne said. "That's where they do all the maintenance on the rides and stuff."

I felt relieved, knowing we'd have some steady work until Conklin's season started up again.

"OK," I said to Layne. "That sounds good."

We hung out in the tent for a few hours. We finished the beer we had in the cooler. Then we went to bed.

In the morning, Layne and I got up early and got ready to go.

"What are we going to do with the cots and the tent and shit?" I said.

We hadn't even taken the tent down yet.

"Ah, just leave it," Layne said.

"Are you sure?" I said.

"Yeah, that shit isn't even mine. The day before we drove up here, I just fucking walked into a Walmart, grabbed a little tent off the shelf, and then walked out of the store with it. Then I went to another store and walked out of there with two cots."

Layne might have been a total thief, but he was a good person to have around, I thought. He was knowledgeable. And if we ever needed money or something, I knew I wouldn't have to worry about it. I knew that Layne would just figure it out.

"All right," I said.

We left the tent there, fully set up, and then we headed over to winter quarters . . .

Florida Crack

It was five o'clock in the afternoon and Layne and I had just gotten off work. All day we'd been sanding the cars for the doppel loop roller coaster.

We left the work area, which was outside, and then went inside, to the office, to get our draws. Every day after work, everyone who wanted a draw—an advance on their next paycheque—could get one.

There was a line of people who wanted to get a draw from the office. Layne and I got into the line.

Layne went first. Then I went in.

Shelley, the broad who worked in the office, was sitting at her desk. "How much do you want?" she asked me.

"A double," I said.

Usually, we could get a draw of twenty or thirty dollars. A double was twenty bucks.

Shelley made a record of it in her book, and then gave

me a twenty-dollar bill.

I walked out of there. Layne was waiting for me outside the door.

As we walked back to our bunk, I started to feel hungry. I was thinking about getting something to eat.

I mentioned this to Layne. Layne had other plans, though. "Let's get some dope," he said.

At first, I thought Layne meant cocaine.

"No, *crack*," Layne said. "You ever smoke crack, Jim?"

"No, I've only ever done freebase," I said.

In Edmonton, Alberta, crack wasn't available before I'd left with the show. You couldn't buy it on the street there. You had to buy cocaine, cook it up with ammonia, and smoke freebase.

"It's just like freebase," Layne said. "The high's the same. You just don't have to bother cooking it up, dealing with ammonia and all that bullshit."

Because I'd never done crack before, I wanted to try it.

"All right," I said.

I gave Layne most of my draw.

"You can just wait in the bunk," Layne said. "I won't be long. I know a guy nearby. He'll come right here to winter quarters."

Layne took off to go get the dope. I went back to our bunk. The bunks at winter quarters were basically right outside, where we worked.

In about half an hour, Layne came back with the dope. It was just one big chunk. It wasn't wrapped up in anything. It was just loose in his pocket.

Layne pulled his duffle bag out from under his bed and started to go through it. He quickly found what he was looking for—a gutted tire gauge.

"I don't have a stem," Layne said. "Most people use stems to smoke crack these days. This thing works fine, though. I'll set everything up for you, OK? You're going to do the first hit."

"OK," I said.

Layne got it all set up. He took some Brillo out of his duffle bag, and then crammed a little piece of it into the end of the tire gauge. Then he broke off a little piece of dope and put it on top of the Brillo.

The next thing he did was take out a matchbook.

"What do you need matches for?" I said. "Why don't you just use a lighter?"

"You don't want to use too much heat when you do this," Layne said.

"Why, does it burn up too fast or something?"

"No, you just don't get as much smoke. Heat is crack's enemy. You're not supposed to keep a flame to it for too long. It's better to use matches because they don't burn as hot as a lighter, and then they burn out."

"Oh. Every time I've done freebase, I've always just used a lighter."

"Well, you're not supposed to do that. You're supposed to use a double match."

Layne lit two matches, and then held them both to the end of the tire gauge. He melted the dope into the Brillo a little bit. The he handed me the tire gauge. I put the end of it to my mouth. Layne lit another two matches. Then he held them to the end of the tire gauge while I inhaled.

I tried to inhale as much as I could and then hold it in my lungs for as long as possible. I knew, from smoking freebase, that the bigger the hit you took, the higher you got.

The high kicked in immediately. It felt just like when I'd done freebase. I got the bell ringer. I broke out in a sweat. The only thing that was different was that I wasn't so shaky. I knew this was because we were in Florida, where the cocaine was a lot purer. It wasn't mixed with speed and all that bullshit, like it was in Edmonton.

We smoked the dope until it was gone. We hung out for a little while after that, and then went to bed.

So, I tried crack, I thought, as I was falling asleep. Well, that was fun.

In the morning, Layne and I went to work. We continued sanding the cars for the doppel loop. That was our job—to sand the cars and then paint them. The cars were old and faded. The reason we were sanding them was to rough them up a bit, so that the paint would stick.

At around noon, we heard this horn beeping, suddenly. It was the food truck. It came by every day, usually around the same time.

Layne and I put down our sanders and went with everyone else over to the food truck. I was starving. I hadn't eaten anything since lunch the previous day.

Because I'd already spent my draw, if I wanted to eat, I had to get food on credit. I didn't want to owe too much to the food truck at the end of the week, so all I got was a ham and cheese sandwich and a drink.

"Anything else?" the guy said.

"No, that's it," I said.

The guy told me the total.

"Can I get it on credit?" I said.

"Sure," the guy said. "What's your name?"

The guy took a notepad out of the apron he was wearing. He pulled a pencil out from behind his ear.

I gave the guy my full name. He wrote it down on his notepad. Then he gave me my food.

I wolfed down the sandwich. I was so hungry that, at first, it felt like I hadn't even eaten anything. I felt like there was still nothing in my stomach. It took a few minutes, but soon, I started to feel better. The food started to absorb and I felt like I'd actually eaten something.

Layne and I hung out by the bunkhouses for a while. Then lunch break ended and we got back to work.

We worked for a few more hours and then we were done for the day.

Once we were done work, everyone who wanted a draw went over to the office again. Layne went in and got his draw. Then I went in and got mine.

As we walked away from the office, Layne turned to me suddenly. "Let's get some drugs again," he said.

I'd had a good time the day before, getting high with Layne. I really liked the crack high. It was such a rush. I'd thought about it a few times during the day, actually. I wanted to do it again.

"Sure," I said. "I need to buy smokes, though."

"All right," Layne said. "Just take out what you need for smokes, and then give me the rest."

I went back to the bunk. Layne went to meet the dealer. When he came back, we got high. I still found it weird using the matches, so Layne lit them for me, and then held them to the end of the tire gauge every time I did a hoot.

After smoking crack a couple of times, Layne and I fell into a routine. Every day after work, we got our draws. Then we got some dope. I knew that I could get food every day on credit, so it didn't bother me, spending my draw every day. Even though it wasn't a lot of food that I was eating at lunch, I found that once I had a little bit to eat, I felt OK.

This routine went on for a couple of weeks.

Then, one day, while I was outside painting one of the cars for the doppel loop, John Taylor walked by. John had a bunch of joints at winter quarters. He was basically partners with Conklin.

"Hey, John," I said.

"Fuck, Jim, look at yourself in the mirror," John said. "You look like shit."

I was shocked. I didn't even know what to say.

John walked away. I went back to work.

Later that day, I went and looked at myself in the mirror.

Wow, I thought. You *do* look like hell.

I'd gotten so thin from not eating properly that my cheeks were sunken in.

The whole time I'd been at winter quarters, I hadn't looked in the mirror very much. I hadn't realized that I'd dropped so much weight. Every day I'd just looked at Layne, and he looked fine. Layne was a lot stockier than I was, though. He could obviously lose quite a bit of weight without it showing on his face.

I started to think about how much dope I'd been using.

Maybe you should slow down a bit, I thought.

The day after John Taylor made this comment to me, winter quarters ended. The show started getting ready to head down to Miami to set up for the Dade County Youth Fair.

Before we left, I got paid for the last week of winter quarters. I gave the office what I owed to the food truck so that they could pay off my bill. Then Layne and I walked over to the fairgrounds, where the South Florida Fair had been held back in January, and picked up our paycheques from the parking crew job we'd worked on.

Layne and I went to a cheque cashing place to cash our cheques. Because I'd gotten the job using a fake American social security number, I was worried there was going to be a problem. The clerk didn't call in the cheque, though. She didn't even ask me for ID, which I found odd.

As soon as we got out of there, I turned to Layne. "I can't believe they didn't even ask for ID," I said.

"They never ask for ID there," Layne said. "And they never call to verify the cheques either. They get so many people cashing cheques there all the time from the parking crew that they know the employer's legit."

I felt relieved to have the money in my pocket.

"You know what we should do?" Layne said.

"What?" I said.

"We should pool our money together and then go buy some weed and some dope as soon as we get to Miami. We can smoke some, sell some, and make our money back."

I knew I'd be making money in Miami, setting up the doppel loop, so it didn't matter to me if I spent the cash. I was just looking to have fun and to party. I didn't really think I had a drug problem. I wasn't too concerned anymore about what John Taylor had said. I had a pocketful of cash and I just wanted to go have some fun with it.

"Sure," I said to Layne. "Sounds like a plan."

We were supposed to go with the doppel loop on the jump to Miami, but Tom Fillmore, who was head of Guest Relations, offered us a ride. "I'm hauling a load there," he told us. "You guys can catch a ride with me, if you want."

Now that Layne and I had plans once we got to Miami,

we wanted to get there as fast as possible. The doppel wouldn't be leaving for a little while.

"Sure," Layne said to Fillmore.

"Yeah, that'd be great," I said.

"All right," Fillmore said. "Go get your stuff."

Brutal Setup

It was the middle of the night and Layne and I were in our bunk, smoking crack. Suddenly, we heard footsteps. They came right to our door.

There was a knock.

"Yeah, who is it?" Layne said.

"It's Mickey," a voice said.

Layne and I were both sitting on the bottom bunk bed. Layne was closest to the door. He got up, unlocked the door, and let Mickey in.

Mickey came into the bunk and pulled the door closed behind him. He reached into his pocket. Then he handed Layne five one-dollar bills.

I figured that after smoking crack all night, this was all the money that Mickey had left.

Layne broke off a little rock and handed it to Mickey.

Mickey left. Layne locked the door.

Before Mickey had shown up, nobody had come to our bunk to buy dope for almost an hour.

"I think they're done for the night," Layne said.

"Yeah," I said. "They must all be broke by now."

Layne picked up the gutted tire gauge that we were using to smoke crack with. He put a rock on the end of it, lit a couple of matches, melted the dope into the screen a little bit, and then did a blast . . .

Soon, I started to hear people talking outside the bunkhouse. People were starting to get up, have coffee, and take showers. Layne and I were still up, getting stoned.

I was wondering what time it was. Layne and I had to be at the ride at nine o'clock.

I glanced at my watch. I couldn't believe it. "Shit," I said to Layne, "it's already nine o'clock!"

Layne had just done a blast and was really stoned and out of it. "Huh?" he said.

"It's nine o'clock, man," I said. "We've got to get to work. Fuck, we should already *be* at work right now."

Layne looked like he didn't give a damn. "Fuck work," he said. "I don't feel like working today, man."

I didn't feel like working either. Neither of us had even slept yet. We hadn't slept for two days. We'd literally been up for two days straight, smoking crack, and selling it to the guys on the show all night out of our bunk.

I decided to follow Layne's lead. I picked up the tire gauge and did another hoot of crack.

I'd no sooner exhaled a huge cloud of crack smoke, when, all of a sudden, someone started pounding on our door. It scared the living shit out of me.

"Layne!" the person yelled. "Jimmy! Get your fucking asses out of there right now. It's time for work!"

It was our boss, Doug Hannigan, the guy who ran the doppel loop roller coaster.

Because I'd literally just done a hit, I was way too fucking stoned to deal with Hannigan. Layne had to do the talking.

"Yeah, just a minute," Layne said. "We'll be right out."

"I'm giving you guys ten fucking minutes," Hannigan said. "In ten minutes, you better be out of that bunk and at the fucking ride."

Layne and I didn't move a muscle until we knew that Hannigan was gone.

As soon as he was gone, I turned to Layne. "Wow, is he ever fucking pissed," I said.

"Yeah, I know," Layne said. "What a bastard."

"Guess we've got to go to work now, huh?"

"Yeah, what a bummer, man. Goddamn . . ."

We stashed our dope and the tire gauge. Then we left the bunk. I was still pretty whacked out when I got outside. Layne was pretty fucked up, too.

Layne hung back to lock the door. I walked on ahead. It was cloudy outside and it was raining a bit. It was just as hot and humid outside as it was in our bunk, though, because the AC wasn't working again, so it made no difference being outside. The bunks were supposed to be air-conditioned, but half the time they didn't fucking work properly.

I walked a few paces and then Layne caught up with me. We walked together from the living compound, where the bunkhouses were located, to the back corner of the midway, where we were going to be setting up the doppel loop.

When we got over there, Doug Hannigan and another

guy, Brian McLean, who was basically second in command to Hannigan, were standing around, waiting for us.

Brian didn't seem too angry or anything. Hannigan, though, was a different story. "First off, where the *hell* were you guys yesterday?" he said.

I tried not to make eye contact with Hannigan. I wasn't high out of my mind by this point or anything, but I was by no means straight.

"We were supposed to start setting up yesterday morning, but you guys never showed up," Hannigan said.

"Sorry, about that," Layne said. "We didn't know we had to be here for setup, Doug."

"What about the day before that, then? You guys were supposed to check in with me when you got here, remember? Why didn't you guys do that?"

"We forgot," Layne said.

This was all bullshit, of course. As soon as Layne and I got to Miami, Layne's friend Ryan picked us up in this white pickup truck, and then we drove to a drug dealer's house in some rural area. Layne went into the house, bought a half ounce of crack and a quarter pound of weed, and then we went back to the lot and smoked dope all night and sold crack and weed to the guys on the show. In the morning, we didn't want to work, we just wanted to keep smoking, so we got the hell off the lot early, before any of the bosses got up. Then we had Ryan drive us around Miami all day while we smoked crack in the truck. We stayed up again all night, doing the same shit.

Hannigan looked thoroughly disgusted with me and Layne. "Yeah, whatever," he said. "Just don't let it happen again. You guys can't just show up whenever the hell you want to around here. When you're supposed to be somewhere, you be there. You got it?"

Layne and I both looked at Hannigan. We nodded and then looked back down at the ground.

"Because of you guys, we're now a day behind schedule," Hannigan said. "So, today, we've got a lot of work to do. The first thing we need to do is get all the blocking out of the possum bellies."

The possum belly was the compartment underneath the tractor trailer.

"OK," Hannigan said. "Let's get started."

Brian went and opened up the first possum belly. It was full to the top with wooden blocks. There were two-by-fours, four-by-fours, six-by-sixes, shims—all different sizes of blocks in there.

Brian, Layne, and I started to unload the blocks. As we took them out, we stacked them in a pile, near where we'd be setting up the ride.

It was so hot and humid outside that as soon as I started working, I started sweating like a pig.

"Holy crap, there's a lot of blocks in this thing," I said to Layne.

"This is just one possum belly," Layne said. "There's like five fucking possum bellies full to the top with blocks just for this ride."

"You're kidding me."

"No, this spot's brutal, man. The lot isn't very level. When we're done setting up the ride, there's going to be tons of blocks on one side of the ride, and on the other side, there's only going to be like a shim."

Hannigan came over to me and Layne all of a sudden. He looked at us. "What the hell are you guys on, heroin?" he said.

"Huh?" I said.

"You guys look like you're all zonked out on something."

"I'm not on heroin," I said.

"Neither am I," Layne said.

"We don't do that shit, man."

"Well, pick up the pace a little bit, then. We've got to get all the blocks out of these possum bellies by the end of the day."

Hannigan got a call on his radio.

"Hey, biotch," some guy said.

Biotch was Hannigan's nickname on the show. You could call him that right to his face, just not in front of any of the local help.

"It's Billy, here. We need the crane."

"All right," Hannigan said. "I'll be right over."

Hannigan turned to me. "Jimmy," he said.

"Yeah?" I said.

"You know the crane signals, right?"

Even though I hadn't worked very long on the carnival, I knew all the hand signals for the crane operator. There were a bunch of them: boom down, boom up, cable down, cable up, extend, or extend the thing but don't boom down. All that shit. Nobody had taught this to me directly, I'd just paid attention on previous setups. I'd always worked in a game, but before we opened, sometimes I'd set up rides for extra money. This was the reason I was even setting up the doppel loop in the first place.

"Yeah, I know the hand signals," I said.

"Good," Hannigan said. "Come on, then. You're coming with me."

Hannigan got into his mini drivable crane. I followed behind him on foot, as he drove over to the big wheel, which was the ride that Billy was working on.

The wheel was a ground mount, so the two major stands that held the whole wheel up had to be erected with the crane. They were assembled on the ground. Hannigan went and just raised them up with the crane.

When the big wheel was done with the crane, Hannigan and I went back to the doppel. I continued to unload the blocks from the possum belly with Brian and Layne.

Then Hannigan got another call. This time it was the Polar Express that needed crane assistance, apparently. Hannigan picked me again. I dragged my ass over to the ride in the rain.

This shit went on all morning. Every twenty minutes or so, Hannigan would get a call on his radio, and then he'd drag my ass over to some other fucking ride that needed help with the crane. It was always something small that needed to be done. And because we had the only drivable crane on the lot, we had to go do it. I was going all over the lot with Hannigan to these other rides. It was a lot of walking. I was sweating fucking bullets, but you couldn't even tell that I was sweating because of the rain.

Finally, we got a break. "Take half an hour for lunch," Hannigan said.

Layne and I went over to the commissary. We each got a coffee and a sandwich. We sat down at a picnic table under a tent and ate our food. While we ate, I bitched to Layne about Hannigan.

"This guy's driving me like a slave," I said.

"Yeah, he's working you pretty hard," Layne said.

"Every time I'm giving him the hand signals for the crane, I just feel like flipping him off. '*Here's* a hand signal for you, buddy!'"

Layne laughed.

"I'm so fucking tired right now," I said. "When I finish work today, I'm just going to fucking crash."

"Me, too," Layne said. "I might not be doing all the running around that you're doing, but I'm a lot older than you, Jim. When you're a teenager, you can stay up for a couple days, you know? It's a lot different when you're fucking pushing thirty."

I didn't say it to Layne at that moment, but, really, I'd already had enough of Hannigan. I was about ready to quit.

If only you hadn't stayed up for two days straight, smoking drugs, I thought to myself, you'd be able to handle this shit right now, no problem.

Under normal circumstances, I would have easily been able to handle all this running around in the heat in Miami. Staying up for two days straight, though, especially while doing heavy drugs the whole time, had really taken a lot out of me. It didn't matter that I was younger than Layne. I'd never gone on a drug binge that had lasted this long before. I felt like I'd pretty well reached my limit. I'd partied, and it had been fun, but I was really paying for it now. I was really dogging it.

"I hope that fucking biotch hires some local help tomorrow," Layne said. "Normally, the show will hire twenty to thirty niggers to set up the doppel. He's just trying to make a point by not hiring anybody today."

"He's punishing us," I said.

"That's exactly what he's doing. The only reason he's riding your ass more than mine, Jimmy, is because you're the new guy. He just wants to see if you can handle it."

Lunch break ended and we had to get back to work.

Layne and I dragged our asses back to the doppel.

In the afternoon, it was more running around in the rain. I was either going to other rides with Hannigan and helping him with the crane, or I was at the doppel, unloading those fucking blocks.

I managed, somehow, to get through the rest of the work day. Finally, it was five o'clock, and the day was done.

Before Hannigan cut me and Layne loose, he bitched at us one last time for being late for work that morning. "I want you guys here at 9 a.m. *sharp* tomorrow," he said.

"OK," I said.

I was so fucking tired that I could barely stand.

"All right," Layne said.

"If I ever have to knock on your door like that again, there's going to be serious fucking trouble. Do you understand?"

"Yeah," I said.

"Yeah, we got it," Layne said.

"OK," Hannigan said. "You guys can go."

As we walked back to the living compound, I suddenly felt this momentary burst of energy. I didn't know where it came from. It felt almost like giddiness or something. I think I was just so glad to be done work that I got almost a rush off of it.

I noticed Layne suddenly pick up the pace. He turned to me as we walked. "As soon as I get out of the shower, I'm doing a huge fucking blast," he said.

"Yeah, me, too," I said.

I suddenly didn't care anymore about the brutal setup I'd just had to suffer through. After all, I'd still managed to get my work done. I might have stayed up for two days straight, smoking drugs, but, in the end, I'd still worked all day like a fucking champ.

"We just won't go as hard tonight," Layne said.

"Yeah, good idea," I said.

But I knew that we would.

"We'll just make sure to get some sleep," Layne said. "As long as we don't stay up all night again, we'll be fine."

"Yeah," I said. "As long as we get a few solid hours of sleep, we should be good."

Welding Lesson

One afternoon, while the show was setting up in Miami, my boss, Doug Hannigan, asked me if I'd help him do some welding. The show had just gotten this new water flume ride. This was the ride with the logs that you sat in and that took you down the little waterfall, and that got you wet. The show had gotten brand new trailers for this ride, so there were no possum bellies underneath them. Most trailers on the carnival had possum bellies to store blocking and what not. So the show asked Hannigan, who was a welder by trade, to construct these things.

"I'll need a helper while I'm welding," Hannigan said to me. "You interested, Jimmy? It'll be a two-day job."

Hannigan wasn't offering me any money to do this, of course. He was just looking for someone to do some free labour. I was still new on the show, though, so I didn't want to say no and be a pain in the ass.

"Yeah, OK," I said to Hannigan. "I'll help you."

My only concern was that I'd never welded before. I'd never even been around other people welding. I didn't know anything about it.

I mentioned this to Hannigan. He didn't seem too concerned. "You're not going to be doing any actual welding, Jimmy," he told me. "I just need you to stand there and hold stuff for me, while I tack weld it."

"Oh, OK," I said.

The next morning, I got up early and went to help Hannigan. The new ride, which was called Niagara Falls, wasn't far from where we'd been setting up the doppel loop roller coaster. We weren't done setting up the doppel yet. Because Hannigan had to construct these possum bellies, we were taking a break from it.

Hannigan and I immediately got to work. What he had me do was hold these sheets of metal with diamond-shaped holes in them. First, he'd tack the sheet to the frame of the possum belly. Once it was tacked on in a couple of places, I didn't have to hold it anymore. It was basically holding its own weight anyway, because it would sit on the frame of the possum belly. I just had to hold it in place for a few minutes, while Hannigan tack welded it, so that it didn't fall over. Once he had the thing tack welded, he just went around it and welded it all.

It was a pretty tedious job. I did this all day, until five o'clock, and then Hannigan told me that we were done for the day.

"Be back here tomorrow at nine," Hannigan said.

"OK," I said.

I went and got something to eat at the cookhouse. I was feeling kind of tired after that, so I went to my bunk and just chilled in there for the rest of the night.

I went to bed that night at around ten o'clock. Sometime during the night, I woke up. My eyes felt weird. They felt a bit itchy.

I didn't think much of it. I just figured that my eyes were irritated for whatever reason. They didn't hurt or anything, they just felt weird.

So, I went back to sleep.

I woke up again at around eight thirty in the morning. I was alone in my bunk. My roommate Owen had already left for work.

It was still nice and dark in the bunk. There was a window on the back wall, but we'd covered it to keep the sun out in the morning.

I sat up in bed. My eyes were really bothering me now. They felt a lot worse than they had in the middle of the night. I felt like I had sand in them or something. Every time I blinked, I felt this gritty sensation. My eyes were also watering like crazy.

My eyes were bothering me so much that I didn't feel like going to work. I knew that I had to go help Hannigan finish the welding, though, so I got my ass out of bed, changed my clothes, and then put on my shoes.

As soon as I opened the door to go outside, I was blinded by the sunlight. I literally couldn't see a thing. All I could see was pure white.

I groaned and then shut my eyes.

The sensation was like when a doctor shined a bright light in your eyes.

A few seconds later, I tried opening my eyes again. The same thing happened. I literally couldn't see a thing.

I started to panic. I thought I'd gone blind.

The worst thing about it all was that I was in a bunk by myself and I couldn't even leave to go get help. I couldn't even walk out of my bunk door because there weren't even any steps there. It was like a catwalk outside the bunks. At the end of the catwalk, was a set of stairs. There weren't even any railings or anything, so I had nothing to hold on to. So I couldn't even leave my bunk.

I heard some voices nearby.

"Hey!" I yelled.

Somebody answered.

"Come over here," I said. "I need help."

Someone came over right away. I didn't recognize the person's voice at first.

"Who's that?" I said.

"It's Steve," the person. "What's wrong?"

"I don't know, man. Something's wrong with my eyes. I can't fucking see."

Steve tried to calm me down. I could tell from his voice, though, that he was pretty freaked out.

"I'll go call someone," Steve said. "Maybe we can get a doctor here."

"Just take me to Hannigan," I said. "I'm supposed to be at work in ten minutes."

"Where's he at?"

"By that new water flume ride we just got—Niagara Falls."

I had to lock my bunk first before we could leave. "Can you get my keys out of my pocket and lock my door for me?" I said to Steve.

Steve got my keys and then locked the door. Then he took me by the arm and guided me along the catwalk. The whole time I was walking, I felt like I was going to fall on my face. I was realizing for the first time, how horrible it was to be blind.

"Watch your step," Steve said. "We're at the stairs now."

"I feel like I'm going to fall," I said.

"No, I've got you. You'll be fine."

I slowly made it down the steps. When we got onto the ground, we walked a few more paces.

"OK, watch your step again," Steve said.

"What's there?" I said.

"You're going to step over a hose."

There were so many hoses and electrical cords all over the ground in the living compound.

I stepped over the hose. A few seconds later, I was stepping over another one.

It took a long time, but we finally got over to the ride.

"OK, here's Hannigan," Steve said. "I've got to go to work now, Jimmy."

Steve let go of my arm.

I heard some footsteps coming toward me.

"What the fuck's this about?" Hannigan said to me. "Why do you have your eyes closed, Jimmy? You know, you're late, by the way."

"I can't fucking see, Doug," I said. "I needed a fucking guide dog just to get me here."

"Shit," Hannigan said. "Were you watching me weld yesterday?"

I couldn't even understand the question. "Of course I was watching you weld," I said. "I was helping you all day."

"No, I mean, were you looking at the actual welding?" Hannigan said. "When I had the torch going, and you were holding the sheets of metal, were you looking down at the flame?"

This was all I'd been doing. Hannigan had never told me not to do this.

"Yeah," I said. "Why?"

Hannigan started to laugh. "Oh, my god," he said. "You're not supposed to do that! Why do you think I wear a helmet when I'm welding? In the future, Jimmy, when you're around someone who's welding, don't ever look at the flame coming out of the torch. That's how you get welder's flash."

Yeah, good advice, I thought.

It was kind of late, though, to tell me this now.

"So, what are you saying?" I said. "Am I going to be fucking blind now? Is this permanent?"

Hannigan laughed again. "No," he said. "You're not going to be blind, kid. Your eyes will be fine. They'll be fine by tomorrow."

I heard a noise like Hannigan had put something down on the ground. My eyes were still closed, so I couldn't tell what the hell was going on around me.

"Hold on," Hannigan said. "I'll be right back."

Hannigan took off for a second. When he came back, he put something in my hand.

It felt like a little plastic bottle or something.

"What's this?" I said.

"Eye drops," Hannigan said. "Put a drop or two in each eye every couple of hours today. It'll keep them from drying out."

"OK."

"I guess you can go back to your bunk now, Jimmy. I'll have to get someone else to help me with the welding today."

Hannigan got someone to bring me back to my bunk. I

had nothing to do in there all day but sit on my bed, in the dark, applying eye drops every couple of hours.

While I sat in bed, I started to stew about Hannigan.

Man, what a fucking asshole! I thought to myself.

I'd watched the guy weld all fucking day and not once did he tell me to look up. Never once did he tell me, "Don't look at the welding."

I knew that Hannigan hadn't actually seen me looking down at the welding because he was paying attention to what he was doing. He could have told me beforehand, though, before we started working, just as a precaution, just in case I didn't know, that I shouldn't look at the flame. I did tell him, after all, that I knew nothing about fucking welding.

As the day went on, my eyes started to feel a bit better. By the time I woke up the next morning, they felt fine.

I opened the door to the bunk and, even though it was really sunny outside, just as Hannigan had told me, I could see perfectly fine . . .

ABOUT THE AUTHOR

S.E. TOMAS, the "street author," is a Canadian fiction author and former carnival worker who sells his novels and short stories on the streets of the Greater Toronto Area. *Carny Short Stories Volume 1* is his third book. He lives in Mississauga.

Also available in paperback

S.E. TOMAS

CRACKILTON

Set in the lower city of Hamilton, Ontario during the global recession of the late 2000s, this novel by S.E. Tomas depicts three and a half months in the life of a seasonally unemployed carnival worker named Jim. Convenience store parking lots, crack houses, and the welfare office are among the places Jim finds himself in this gritty, darkly funny, and compassionate story about a blue-collar guy struggling with crack addiction.

TORONTO'S STREET AUTHOR

Also available in paperback

S.E. TOMAS

SQUEEGEE KID

Squeegee Kid is the story of a twenty-one-year-old carnival worker who winds up stranded, homeless, and living in a shelter in the downtown core of Toronto, Ontario. Based on S.E. Tomas's own experiences in the '90s, and told from the perspective of Jim, his fictional alter ego, this autobiographical novel offers a raw first-person account of life on the streets of Canada's largest city.

TORONTO'S STREET AUTHOR